THE LAST LIGHT

D1569054

THE LAST LIGHT

a novel by

ELIZABETH SANDERS

—

FALL 2015
BROKEN LEVEE BOOKS
an imprint of CHIN MUSIC PRESS
SEATTLE

PUBLISHER:
Chin Music Press
1501 Pike Place #329
Seattle, WA 98101
USA

www.chinmusicpress.com

Library of Congress Cataloging-in-publication data is available

For B.
and my brothers

One more such victory and we are lost.
—King Pyrrhus, 280 BCE

Oleum camino addere
—Erasmus

Someone is singing Silent Night.

Same damn thing every year.

This is the last year, Walter promises himself. The last damn year he comes to this place. He's been saying this for the past twenty. He saws a wedge in a willow log, fits a smaller piece into its cut groove. He pauses to zip his fleece, pull down his camouflage hat. In the distance, passing somewhere north of them, a rusty freight train fumbles towards the smoke-billowing chimneys of petrochemical plants.

When Walter Doucet was young, six or seven, he remembers asking Dad, "What's the point of spending so much time building something, just to burn it down?"

"You just," Dad replied. The grinding saw said the rest.

Forty-seven years later, Dad a year gone, and Walter is still hammering together a wooden teepee on the levee across from his grandparents' empty house in Vacherie, Louisiana.

All along the Mississippi River from New Orleans to Baton Rouge, fires are lit. Feux de Joie, it's called. The fires guide the ghosts of midnight travelers down the river to mass. They light the way for Papa Noel and his gators in this swampy pit of Earth, Gaston, Tiboy, Pierre, Alcee—

Walter is handed another cut log to fit in the pyre.

"You heard from him," a cousin asks.

"Not yet," Walter says.

Cousins, nephews, friends of the family, mostly men, work to gather good wood, find the best fillers. Officially, the wood is found from the first day after Thanksgiving until Christmas Eve morning, when the men go out just after dawn and begin to build their pyre.

Unofficially, Walter gathers one item a little earlier than that. Palm Sunday. Dried palm fronds make excellent fire fuel, better than newspaper. He attends three services that day, filling his trunk each time. They are his symbol of victory and triumph. Presumptuous? Usually.

"What's he doing?" another cousin asks.

"Not sure," Walter says. He watches the road for his brother's sports car.

Yesterday afternoon was the last time he heard from Collins. Walter hadn't picked up the call. Collins hadn't left a message.

"Maybe this year it's just one," says Tut, his second cousin with a round face and a confidently-shaped beard. He pats Walter on the shoulder.

When Walter was seventeen and Collins twenty-one, the bonfire torch was passed down from Dad and Uncle Wilvin. A fight broke out and one fire became two competing fires. Dad sided with Collins; Uncle Wilvin with Walter.

The rules are simple. The wood has to be found. Nothing in the ground can be uprooted for the sole purpose of burning it. Money is arbitrary. Man-made material, forbidden.

"Get me a beer, will ya?" Walter says.

He checks his phone. No messages. He starts in on another willow log. Slowly his pyre is taking shape.

Building a bonfire seems easy. Good fire wood, solid pyre.

The wood needs to be dry. It should burn evenly without any sparks and little smoke. Ideally it will burn for a long time, with what's known as strong "coaling qualities" or oxidation rates.

But as with any element, control is not the word for what is obtained.

Large boys in hunting fleece and scruffy faces haul loads from the back of pickup trucks. A small group of men gather on the levee, camping out on orange coolers. Collins's crew.

One of them mouths to Walter, "Where is he?" and points to his watch.

Walter shrugs. Collins is late. No surprise there.

When the men aren't looking, Walter checks his phone again, no messages. He goes to dial Collins's number but stops. He puts the phone back in his pocket.

As Grandpaw used to say, "You can't put out water with fire."

As a nephrologist at Touro Hospital, Walter is needed when the body, for some reason, is unable to adjust its physiological process to maintain internal equilibrium. Something is off with its secretion, selective retention. Elimination.

Electrolytes. Solutes. Sodium, glucose, glutamate. Water.

He knows these things.

But by Friday, December 2nd, any attempts of personal homeostasis have failed.

His wife, Phoebe, is directing another one of her misguided silent treatments at him. And Collins keeps calling him about random stuff, like did Walter remember the name of Dad's old war buddy. Or what was the name of the movie with such-and-such actor. Or if Walter needed any bulk from the Sam's Club.

"No, thanks, nothing for me," Walter says, not putting up a fight, or "I've never actually seen that movie," or "Dad never had that conversation with me."

Walter pushes the needle-like nephroscope through a small incision in an orange, antiseptic circle on the patient's flank for a fairly routine percutaneous nephrostolithotomy. He instructs a resident on how to guide the scope, adjusts the lens and watches the camera make its way toward the kidney.

"Continue along this path?" a resident asks as she guides the nephroscope. She's a short woman whose face seems stuck on the verge of smiling.

"About fifteen degrees to the left," Walter says.

The team huddles around the metal table, watching the small screen as the camera burrows through layers of bumpy yellow and foam-like pink, through pulsing red and raw gray. This isn't the patient's first kidney stone, but it's the first to be so aggressive against less invasive treatments.

Walter glances through the objective lens. Each kidney is surrounded by a thick layer of adipose tissue called perirenal fat, which helps protect it. A tough, fibrous connective tissue, the renal capsule, envelopes each kidney, providing support for the soft tissue inside. "Now about four degrees to the right," he says.

The stone, easily 2.2, 2.4 centimeters appears. Walter studies the crystal formations: calcium oxalate with surface folds like fool's gold or a forest fungus. Stalactites or stalagmites, the difference? This always finds its way into Walter's head when he enters the cave of the kidney.

"Looks good," he says and instructs the new resident on how to thread the ultrasonic probe through the nephroscope. "Kalman, how many degrees and in what direction?"

"Ten degrees south, sir."

"Ding, a year's supply of Kibbles for you," Walter says. No one laughs.

The glass OR doors slide open again, "Dr. Doucet." It's the same nurse from before. "Your brother wanted me to tell you that it wasn't urgent, no emergency. Just call him back when you get the chance."

"Thank you," Walter says, having figured as much.

A beep alerts them to the machine's readiness, Walter orders an ultrasonic pulse released into the kidney.

When Walter was still in med school, he remembers eating fried oysters with Dad and Collins at a dive shack in Cut Off during a fishing trip. A man sat next to their table trying to chew fried catfish with a toothless mouth. He smelled of something sweet and sour like milk left in the sun too long. His kidneys were failing. That's what they were smelling. The yellowing of the skin. The permanent dampness on the neck and cheeks.

"—Fragmentation failed," says a resident with a moon-shaped, cratered face.

"Move ten point six degrees north of the stone," Walter orders. They increase the machine's frequency fourteen hertz, release two pulses.

"A piss doctor?" he can still hear Dad say. "Why the hell would you want to be a piss doctor?"

"Fragmentation failed," a resident says.

Walter regains focus and takes over. He moves four degrees northwest, ups the machine ten hertz, and releases a long pulse.

An adult human kidney is only about 12 cm long, 6 cm wide, 3 cm thick, and yet 300 milliliters of blood flow through them each minute. Four hundred gallons a day. Four hundred. The internal plumbing of the kidney stretches five hundred miles. Almost a quarter of the river's length.

"—Dr. Doucet, Dr. Doucet," a resident's hand is on his shoulder. Walter quickly lets go of the machine. "We have fragmentation."

"Correct," Walter says. He can feel his neck flush. "Thread the nephrostomy tube and watch that it drains. I have to make a call."

The hall smells of false pine and ammonia. Walter leans against the vending machine, his forehead vibrating against the cold plastic. He digs in his pocket for change and is a quarter short. He stays there, pressing the buttons.

"Walter?"

"Dr. Erickson," he says to the new urologist. He's the young, fresh blood the hospital is trying to recruit. Before Touro, he'd done a stint in El Salvador and published a study from it. His hair is long, and he wears hip dress shirts with bow ties from the Salvation Army.

"Did you have a chance to look at that chart?" Walter asks.

"Ah, I'm moving a little slow this morning. My wife's book club ran late last night," he says with a wink. Walter knows he's not married and has no clue what this is code for. This is my competition, Walter thinks, this kid.

"The chart, Dr. Erickson," Walter says and walks back down the corridor.

In his office, Walter calls his brother.

"Guess what I'm doin' right now?" Collins says.

"I don't know, what?" Walter feels unusually spent.

"Guess."

"I'm in surgery. What?"

"Why'd you call if you were in surgery? Jesus, Walt, you coulda called me back later."

"Just what, I'm on the phone now, so, what?"

"I'm in front of a machine that's cleanin' my balls and fillin' my mug." Collins is a golfer.

"You couldn't wait to say that, could you?"

"Well, I could've waited 'til you were out of surgery."

"Bye, Collins."

"Wait. I need you to go out to the house with me this weekend. We've got to start cleaning it out."

"I can't."

"You owe me, Walt."

"For what?"

"Do not make me do it alone."

"Fine."

"Yeah?"

"OK," Walter finds himself saying, too weak to argue.

Before rounds, Walter checks on the patient in the OR, a Mr. J.R. Marny. Two attending nurses watch the tube drain and adjust his oxygen mask.

Walter picks up the plastic bag hanging from the tube; it's filled with cloudy urine, traces of blood, and stone fragments. He turns on the objective lens.

"Should I page a resident?" A nurse asks.

"No, I'm just going to finish up here." Walter likes when the room is near empty and quiet, except for the hum and whir and beep of the machines, a sterile symphony. Through the microscope, he scans the kidney for any remaining stone fragments.

He can still hear the sounds of black and white westerns leak in from the den. Walter is a boy sitting next to Grandmaw at the kitchen table as she cross-stitches the same pattern into a small square of rough cloth, over and over. A wide-eyed rabbit in brown thread. She clamps the square onto a jar of something pickled, lines them up to be gifted for a couple's marriage, the birth of a child, a new job, the loss of someone.

If pluses are brown and circles are light brown, it starts, a row of pluses, then a row of circles, circle, plus, plus, plus. Then circle, circle, plus, plus. He knows the pattern, sometimes recites it in his head when he's doing double-back sutures on a patient's flank.

"Should we get you an apron?" Dad used to say to him on his way to the refrigerator.

Should we get you an apron? Something still tightens in Walter. He injects the hemostatic sealant down the nephrostomy tract to the kidney. Should we get you an apron? How about a doctor's coat. Walter removes the guidewires, the tube. He begins the double back of two small sutures.

He pulls the thread tight while a nurse cuts. "Let's move him to a room."

When the nurses begin to remove the patient from the machines, Walter feels a suffocating sensation that cuts into his breath much lower than the lungs.

WALTER IS STUCK IN SOME SICK agrarian cycle: bury, return. Burn. Return. He is suffocating under soil. Spit out. Swallowed whole.

"Remember when Dad got up to 105 on this road in that truck of his?" Collins says on Sunday as they make the drive from New Orleans to Vacherie. They were supposed to leave before noon. Collins didn't show until after three. "Remember?"

"No, I don't," Walter says.

"Maybe you weren't there."

"Maybe not." This is how they reminisce about Dad.

Walter listens to the seat belts slap the backseat and thinks of Dad's '78, blue Ford truck. None of them were small enough to fit comfortably in the back seat. Usually just one of them rode passenger with him.

Walter looks at Collins. His light blue polo is wet in the armpits. They have the same dark hair, but Collins's is thinning at his widow's peak. Collins is thicker than Walter, who's three inches taller.

"Anything exciting in nephro-land?" Collins always thinks he wants to talk about Walter's work, until they actually do.

"I removed a stone last week that was almost half an inch long."

Collins nods his head, tries to look interested.

"It was lodged in the upper track of his urethra."

"OK, OK."

"Imagine trying to pass that."

Collins winces. He grabs his crotch and grunts an uncomfortable laugh. This is them bonding.

"Got my handicap down to fourteen last month at this resort in

Perdido," Collins says.

"Great," Walter says, though he has no idea if it is.

"I don't know, maybe it was just the course."

"Maybe not."

Collins works in oil like Dad. He's on the sales end though, so his salary is three times what Dad's had been. "You took it and you ran with it," Dad used to say, proud of the opportunity he thought he'd provided for him.

They drive for a while in silence. Collins puts on the radio, some disco song. Walter changes the station, early rock-in-roll. Collins turns it off.

All along river road is a sweet and bitter smell like seared lost bread. They pass burning fields being cleared for next year's sugar cane harvest. Walter watches the smoke rise, signaling, the end is only the beginning.

"Why'd you tell Wilvin you weren't doing the bonfire?" Collins says. He props his left leg against the door and drives like Dad used to.

"Because I'm not doing it."

"Were you going to tell me?"

"I've told you."

"You have to do it."

"I'm not." The car swerves a little each time Collins looks at Walter, tries to lock eyes.

"Because Dad's gone?"

"Because I'm done."

Collins takes a long, corny philosophical pause before saying, "But it's what we do."

Walter shrugs. "Watch the road."

They pass an armadillo, decapitated, browned by the sun. Walter sees Dad on the hospital bed, deteriorating faster than a spoiled banana. Doctors at Touro ran around trying to figure out what was wrong. "Maybe it's the kidneys?" The kidneys were fine.

"What good is it having a doctor for a son if he can't do anything?" Dad said. The kidneys were fine, were even donated when the heart stopped.

The house, built by their great grandfather, sits dilapidated, open like

16

a geriatric mouth with windows bare and walls crumbling. It's a one-story, Acadian house made of brick, cypress, plaster and mud. It's raised high on masonry foundations, the porch supported by similar columns. The roof is steeply pitched. Walter and Collins spent a good deal of time living here. Raising two boys left Dad without many options.

Tall reeds scrape the sides of the car as they pull into the driveway overgrown with prairie grass.

"Must have been a storm," Walter says. Torn-down tree limbs scatter the yard. Instinctively, Walter thinks, thick branches, but would they dry in time? Raw materials, an inescapable frame of mind.

"You see that?" Collins says, getting out of the car.

"Too wet?"

"That." He points to the remains of an animal curled in the driveway, so decomposed they can't tell what it is. So rotted, it's lost the stench of death. Only a few flies remain to attack the sun-dried tendons still clinging to the bone.

"Don't touch it," Walter finds himself saying, as if it is something they could disturb.

They step on the porch and the boards feel ready to give. Two of the front windows are broken. A fan, hanging by a tethered cord, is no longer anchored to the ceiling. Dead moths cake the inside of a burnt-out Bevolo lantern above the door. An old soda can and candy bar wrapper blow around with dried leaves and dust.

"It's like the inside of your head," Walter says.

"Prick." Collins opens an envelope he pulls from his back pocket. Shakes out a key.

"Where'd you find a key?" Walter asks.

"The lawyer."

"What lawyer?"

The key is unnecessary. The slightest bit of Collins's weight against the door slides it open.

"After you," Collins says because he's always been a bit chickenshit.

In the foyer, collapsing plaster exposes the ceiling's beams. There is an active silence, one beyond the senses. The air is thick and stale and difficult to breathe, but it is still home.

Walter hangs his jacket on the third hanger from the left of the hall tree. Slides his boots next to the umbrella bucket. Smells for dinner. Wishes for ham hocks. Calls for Grandmaw. Hopes Collins isn't home yet from baseball practice. Listens.

Habit, memory's blackening tabernacle, as Grandmaw used to say.

"You smell that?" Collins asks as he pushes past Walter and into the living room. It's a cacophony of rot, mold, dust, dank, and sour. All flooding together and rushing at them. They move the collars of their shirts to barricade their faces.

The dining room windows are shattered. Maybe blown out from a storm, maybe from the same people who took the table. Chairs circle an empty space. "Who steals a table and not its chairs?" Walter says.

"Ah the riddle," Collins says while he fools around with the Victrola lid that never wanted to stay up. "Who takes a piano and not a Victrola?" The piano's frame is outlined on the carpet.

"I though that piano was taken while Dad was still here. His cousin took it. You know the one, elfish head."

"Oh yeah, Dean."

The walls and the floors have swollen and buckled with water damage. Something has feasted on the drape's fabric.

"What if there's a squatter in here?" Walter says.

"Two against one. We're the threat."

"Unless he's armed."

"We could be armed."

"Should be."

Collins pats his pocket. "Swiss army."

"Great, really that's great. Just great."

They walk down the hall and stop at Dad's room. Neither one of them steps in. The sounds of their breathing both turn heavy. From the doorway, Walter sees a pair of Dad's pants draped over a chair by the closet. His clothes hang limp on metal hangers. Tattered shoes with holes in most of the toes are stacked in a messy pile. A mini-decanter wrapped in duct tape, the official spit cup, still sits on the nightstand.

Blood pulses in Walter's ears. He can't get himself to go in.

Collins steps away from the door. "Just do the bonfire."

"No."

"Why?"

"It's too much work."

"It's because you're scared."

Walter gently pushes Collins towards the room. Collins tries to do the same to him.

Walter breaks loose and walks on to the kitchen. Collins follows behind him.

Dust covers everything. It coats the furniture in a gray film. Their footprints are tracked along the pine floors, beside smaller imprints.

The earth is slowly eating the house. Ashes to ashes.

In the kitchen, the tops of the counters and the cabinets are eroded. Rusted, yellow formica and greening wood. Furry cans of tomato juice, pineapple chunks, vienna sausages, and coffee grinds sit stale on a shelf that has lost its doors.

Small footprints are pressed along the lip of the sink. The porcelain base, a mass grave of fruit flies. The kitchen table of strong cypress is tipped on its side, two legs broken.

"Can I have the table?" Walter says.

"It's broken."

"So."

"You gonna burn it?"

"Fix it."

"We'll see."

"Why do you get to decide?"

Collins ignores him, digs in the pantry.

"I became a surgeon at that table," Walter says and immediately regrets it.

"A what? I don't want to know what you did on that table."

"Never mind."

"You can have the damn table, okay? Just keep the rest of it in your hope chest." Collins opens up empty canisters and drops them on the floor of the pantry.

Walter kneels down by the table, sees the rot. It's beyond repair. "What are we even looking for?"

"What's left," Collins says and kicks open the back door, busting one of the hinges. From the back steps, he says something about renting a dumpster.

Walter sits on the back steps. Collins picks up a ball with busted yarn from the grass and tosses it in the air a few times, pretends he's going to pitch it hard at Walter.

"Put it down," Walter says but Collins doesn't. He looks at the screened-in porch off to the right where they used to sleep as boys. He can see their old bunk beds, unstacked, old mattresses sagging in the wire frames. In between the beds is their old chest of drawers. Walter wants it but he doesn't dare say it. He doesn't even have any grandkids to give it to. If anything Collins should get it for his grandson.

Collins holds the ball by the yarn and begins popping it at Walter. It hits his shoulder with a sting.

"Cut it out."

"Say you'll do the bonfire," Collins says and does it again.

"Stop."

"Make me." He does it again.

Walter catches the ball. He pegs it as hard as he can at Collins's leg.

"What the hell did you do that for?" Collins says, rubbing his thigh.

In the yard rot old tires and a tractor, missing its steering wheel.

"This is so typical of him," Walter says. "To leave this for us to clean up."

"You want a beer?" Collins says. "I've got a cooler in my trunk."

They stand on the levee across the road from the house. The bonfire battleground. The day is disappearing into a graying sky. Walter watches a barge push its way down the river, lights blinking, until it becomes the only measurement of time.

"It pisses me off to see the house like that," Collins says. He stands too close to Walter, sipping his beer. He says this every year.

"Why, you want it? You gonna fix it up, put your pretty little wife in it?" Walter says this every year too.

In their dust-covered clothes, they stare at the house, sipping their beers in silence. The river rushes alongside them in a steady, patient stride.

"Walt, the house is mine."

"Take it. Leave me some of the furniture." Walter drains the last of his beer.

"I'm serious. The lawyer called me. Dad left it to me."

"What?" Walter says. "Why?"

"Dunno. He just did. It's in his will."

"How long have you known?"

"A couple months." Collins kicks a stick down the levee.

"Why?" Walter says again, almost shameful.

"Dunno." Collins keeps his gaze on the house. It makes Walter want to punch him. An image rushes at Walter and he feels his eleven-year-old self standing at the bottom of the levee, barefoot on something prickly. In front of him, Collins bounces back and forth with his fists up. Dad yells behind them, at Walter, "Put 'em up. Put your dukes up." But Walter's arms are too heavy. And if he could have, it would have only been to wipe the blood from his nose.

"What are you going to do with it?" Walter asks.

"Dunno."

"Stop saying that." Walter thinks of the black mud at the bottom of the river that releases nothing. He listens to the churning water and finds it almost violent, crashing against itself, against the banks that contain it.

Walter walks down the levee and towards the car. Without thinking, he begins to gather the wet branches in the yard.

"You can't bring those in my car."

"Pop the trunk," Walter says, his insides surging.

"No."

"Pop the damn trunk. I'm not leaving these behind."

Collins unlocks his door, gets in and starts the car.

The branches are too wet to use, but Walter can't back down. Collins shakes his head and begins to pull out of the driveway.

Walter throws the branches in the direction of the car. They miss and tumble down the driveway.

Collins starts down the road. Walter chases the car. He catches up as Collins slows down and tries to open the door. It's locked.

"You ass," Walter says and smacks the window.

"Don't do that to my car." Collins stops the car with a jerk and unlocks the door.

"They were too wet," Walter says.

"I know," Collins says.

The tires kick up dirt behind them as the car speeds down the road. They drive with the windows down, blaring something almost patriotic.

They make their way on the Destrehan Swamp Bridge that sits on stilts in an endless stretch of green-coated water. Nobody wants to go off the road here.

"Winner takes the house," Walter says. "Winner takes it all. Loser never comes back."

"The fire that burns the longest," Collins says like he's got something in mind.

They shake on it.

Walter watches the headlights travel in front of the car. For a second, they shatter the blackness to reveal a crushed opossum.

Walter doesn't want that house. He just doesn't want Collins having it. All he can think of is burning it to the ground. Best damn bonfire there ever was.

A shadow becomes a cypress then turns back into the night. Solid land shows itself only to be a bog. All around them is sinking soil and dark waters.

A TRAIN ORNAMENT ON THEIR TREE makes Walter think of the fifth element, the medium of sound. The Aether, the Void, the Akasha. He is waiting for Phoebe's response. He's told her about the condition of the house. The bonfire. He's left out the house-as-wager detail.

The electric wheels grind the train into the mountain and out, around and around, stuck on an endless track in a tiny globe. The ornament plugs into a bulb socket of the lights. Anywhere he stands in the living room, any time the lights are on Walter hears the damn thing. But he can't ever find it. If he could, he'd unplug it.

"I've always loved that house," Phoebe says. She squats on the living room floor in her sweatsuit, wrapping the presents she pulls from two big shopping bags.

"What would you do with that house?" He tries to tease, but it sounds in some way, accusatory.

"It has so much potential," the realtor in her says.

She tries to fit snow-flaked paper around an oddly-shaped collection of cologne, tube socks, and Mexican coffee beans. The kind Walter likes. She's wrapping his gift.

He sits on a chair next to her. There is not an inch of the living room undecorated. It used to take her and the girls one night of staying up late to get the house "holiday-ready." It's taken Phoebe two weeks of going at it alone.

The paintings on the wall have been changed to the Christmas-themed ones. The tree, ten feet tall and full, is decorated with tinsel and ribbon, lights and bells. And ornaments. Some older than Walter.

On the coffee table is proudly displayed the antique nativity scene, handmade by Phoebe's grandfather. Over the years, the faces of the barn animals have fallen victim to various pets. The baby Jesus kidnapped. Mary, Joseph, and the wise men maimed.

"Remember the year that we first had both of the girls," Phoebe begins. She's struggling being a first-semester empty nester. Her baby, Jolie, is a freshman at Tulane. Their oldest, Claudine, is twenty-four, newly married.

Walter knows she's going to tell the story of the stolen candy cane. He wants her to tell the story of the toy drum, when they were older. He can still hear the thump, can still feel it.

If a sound is felt, not heard, somewhere else in the body, seemingly unregistered in the ears, do the eardrums still beat? What else do we hear as feeling? The twitch of a muscle that won't relax. Who is calling? The sound waves we catch in our gut, what thoughts are being sent on a frequency that have no words to decipher them?

Phoebe uses scissors to scrape along the ribbon. When she releases it, the ribbon tightly curls. She stacks his gift on top of the pile.

"Why is it," Walter tries to change the subject, "that I can know what you are wrapping but as soon as you tie that last string it becomes something else, anything? A package of anything."

"You saw what it is," she says without looking up.

"Not tonight it isn't. Not until Christmas. It's, it's..."

"Something better?"

"I always need socks. I've got a hole in ones I'm wearing right now."

"They aren't for you."

"Every gift under that tree could be for me." Walter stops. She used to laugh when he'd act like this.

Phoebe pulls another box from the bag and begins to wrap it. "Remember when," she starts in again.

Their conversations are just landfills with them rummaging around.

Walter listens to the steady, mechanical hum of the train ornament. After a while, the sound becomes imperceptible. It seems to disappear into some fifth element of nothingness.

Maybe it is where language meets sound only felt.

During the night, Walter has a recurring dream. He is standing in the lobby of a movie theater; he is both young and old. Instead of a concession stand, there is a machine with a rotating conveyor belt that slides toward a metal box, similar to airport security screeners, but larger. Whatever goes in comes out packaged as a small box, the size of a red and white popcorn container with lid flaps that fold into each other. Except for these boxes are gray and don't say Popcorn. They hold the remains of former selves.

Walter waits anxiously in line while the significance of this action doesn't seem to register for everyone else.

"We are not just going into the theatre," Walter says to a dismissive line. They continue to stand as if waiting to choose between diet or regular, chocolate-covered or salted.

And when it is their turn to lie down on the conveyor belt, a sense of contentment relaxes their faces. To them, this rite of passage reveals only hope on its way to unseen nothingness.

Walter feels each one ground into ash. Each small, suffocated breath packaged tight into a container that drops out at the end of the conveyor, indistinguishable from the others.

"There's no coming back," Walter says to the person in front of him, but the connection with the final container is not made. The next person climbs on to the moving belt.

Walter steps out of line. The others look at him in disbelief, How could he try to take this from them?

Walter goes to say, There's no undoing what's done. But once out of the line, he no longer grasps the situation.

Walter wakes in the middle of the night with such an intense weight on him that it takes a few minutes to realize he has to urinate.

He watches the stream hit the water, some splashing on the seat, and he realizes what day it is. December fourth, nine days into official bonfire building season, and he hasn't gathered a single piece of wood.

In the dark, he finds his way back to the bed.

He lies there unable to sleep. He can't stop thinking about the year Collins and Dad painted each of their logs with a combustible lacquer. Maybe it was '86 or '87. Their pyre nearly exploded when they lit it. Some of their crew went to the hospital with minor burns.

They were disqualified.

Walter and Wilvin won by default. Their pyre, a sad attempt of a sleigh replica, burned for less than an hour before collapsing in on itself and dying.

AUTOMATION. SELF-REGULATION. People take for granted the body's involuntary response of expulsion. Until it fails.

The kidneys are the most transplanted organ worldwide. The first successful transplant was in 1954 in the United States between two identical twins. Before the advent of immunosuppressants, twins were the ideal candidates for the procedures.

On Monday, during rounds, Walter finds Mr. Marny propped up by a couple of pillows in his hospital bed, arguing with a nurse about wanting a milkshake. He is a thin man with gray tufts of hair coming out of his large ears and a big, curving nose.

Walter opens his chart and pulls out a checklist he's supposed to run through after a recent lecture by Dr. Erickson about doctors being friends that heal. Building better patient-care skills: describe in layman's terms, simplifying until patient clearly understands prognosis.

"Your urine is alkaline and it tested positive for urease-producing bacteria, known as Proteus. We are going to put you on a strong antibiotic and urease inhibitor. We also need to restrict your diet."

A blank face stares at him.

"We removed the stones from your kidneys," Walter tries again. "We are going to put you on medication. You will need to watch what you eat."

"Can I get a milkshake?"

"No," Walter says. "I'll have a nurse print a list of the foods to avoid."

Walter then pulls from the file a chart with varying faces of discomfort. When asking about pain in different areas of his body, he has Mr. Marny point to the chart. This is also the workings of Dr. Erickson.

"This is bullshit," Dad had said when the doctors gave him the chart. "I hope this hospital is run better than a second grade classroom." He then pointed to the wincing face that said moderate pain for every question asked.

"Now," Walter says, following the checklist, "How would you describe your emotional state today? Is it differing from what you would consider your normal state?" There's a chart for him to point to for this as well. Mr. Marny points to the head that is neither smiling nor frowning. Fine. Neutral.

"This is normal?" Walter asks.

Mr. Marny shrugs.

In Chinese medicine, depression, coping difficulties, and a sense of foreboding are thought to result when the blood is not filtered or warmed enough by the kidneys. They are the organs most associated with the water element. Metaphorically, they supply the energy needed to move forward in life.

Walter writes out a prescription. "I'm going to put you on a drug called—"

"—Zeus?"

And even though the checklist highlights humor as a great way to communicate with a patient, Walter quietly says, "No, sir."

"Jack. Call me Jack."

"Jack, have you arranged for someone to pick you up?"

"I'll have you call me a taxi."

"We recommend that you call someone who can help get you settled at home. Your movement will be more limited than you think."

He doesn't respond, so Walter says, "We have a hospice van—"

"I don't need a damn hospice van. I'm not an invalid."

"Of course not, sir."

"Jack."

"Jack, I'll have the nurses help you set up your ride," which meant they'd give him two options: the hospice van or someone he knows. "Feel better," Walter says and shakes his hand.

Walter still goes back and looks at Dad's chart occasionally. He had symptoms characteristic of something being wrong with the kidneys: profuse sweating, itchy back, pain in the lower back, swelling of the face especially around the eyes, weakness, shortness of breath. But his electrolytes were only slightly out of balance. His blood tests showed no elevation of BUN or creatinine. There was no protein found in his urine.

What was failing couldn't be detected.

Walter sits on a bench outside of the hospital, watching people walk in and out. Each time the doors slide open a draft of cool, sterile air seeps over him. He takes a sip of coffee and a bite of a plastic-wrapped pastry from the vending machine.

Walter tries not to think of the paper he abandoned years ago, Therapeutic Methods for Struvite Nephrolithiasis, in which he focused on controlling stones through the liver's production and oral intake of oxalates as opposed to focusing solely on the intake of calcium or the crystals that form once the urine reaches the kidney. At the time, he was at the forefront of his field. But the study lost funding, the paper never got finished, and the rest of the field caught up.

Walter forces himself to think of something else. The bonfire. How would he build it? He considers a pyre within a pyre. If one structure collapsed or extinguished, the other would still be there. If both lit, it could be twice as strong.

A hospice van pulls up to the far curb and waits. Through the sliding glass doors, a heavy-set nurse wheels out Jack Marny. She keeps calling him "Sugar."

Jack grips closed the neck of his red-striped housecoat. In his lap is a pile of toiletries. The nurse stops to pick up each item that falls. A stick of deodorant, itch cream, a Band-Aid. "Sugar, you gonna need that," she says.

"Leave it," Walter hears Jack say. "Just leave the damn thing."

They go a little farther then something else drops. "I got it, Sugar." She uses the handles of the wheelchair to help herself back up.

Mr. Marny's expression no longer looks neutral. Walter would point to the face that says discomfort. Or if there was a face for it, discontentment.

As they wait for the van's ramp to lower, slowly and loudly, Jack slumps down in the chair and puts his face in his hand. Disgust.

It takes twenty-five minutes to load him before they drive off.

There are many theories as to why humans develop two kidneys when the body can live with just one. The Akkadians in 1700 BCE explained the reason for two kalāte is one to give good advice and the other bad.

Walter throws away his trash and buttons his doctor's coat. If he's going to build a fire that burns the longest, it can't be some fancy structure. It needs to stand alone. It doesn't need a second to catch it, or to cause it all to burn too quickly or sporadically. He needs to focus on the wood. He needs to build it so that when it begins to fall, it still burns.

I N THEIR YARD IS A SWEETGUM tree. The flaming tree, as Walter calls it. In the fall it turns red, yellow, orange, crimson, purple, a smoky brown. The leaves don't just look like fire—it's a full explosion.

It's classified as a hardwood, but the wood is brittle and the tree drops its branches easily in a storm. Which is what Walter was hoping when he planted it twenty-five years ago. The problem has always been they water-log too quickly and are useless in a bonfire.

And for a large portion of the year, the lawn is covered with its prickly seed pods that don't burn that well and are annoying to step on.

Walter tries to kick the pods off the driveway. There are too many of them. A storm from the night before had knocked down a bunch of branches. Walter picks one up that is heavy with water. He drops it.

He grabs the mail and is half-way up the walk when he hears, "Uncle Walt?"

He turns to find a young man, mid-to-late twenties, getting out of a truck.

"What a storm last night, right?" the man says like he knows him. He doesn't. "We had three power lines down by us." He's a fairly big guy, brawny arms and chest. He wears a white, wrinkled T-shirt, faded green cargo pants, and worn hiking boots. "Looks like it took your tarp clean off."

The carport cover flaps over the driveway, a loose rope flying about. There is a two-foot tear where it ripped. "Looks like it," Walter says. "Can I help you?" he says and inspects the guy closer.

His face is full, framed by straight brown hair that comes down over his ears and long bangs swept to the side. His skin has a reddish tan, darkened in areas from conjoined freckles. A couple days of stubble dots his square jaw. He has big, apologetic eyes.

"Uncle Walt, right?"

"Yeah?"

"Ben," he sticks out his hand for Walter to shake. "Ben Guidry."

The knuckles of his hands are red and raw. When Walter notices the grease burn scars on his forearm, he starts to put it all together. "Boon? Boon who makes the mean boudin."

"Yes, sir," Boon says with unguarded pride.

He's dating Uncle Wilvin's granddaughter, Alma. They've been together just eight months and he's already proposed to her, unsuccessfully, twice. Kid wants in bad, Uncle Wilvin said.

Walter's girls played with Alma when they were young, before she started smoking and wearing dark black eye liner and doing whatever else she did.

"What can I do for you?" Walter says.

"You've got a downed gutter too, Boss." He points to the side of the house. "Saw it when I was pulling up."

They walk up to the porch and lean against the railing to look. Sure enough, the whole left side of the garage gutter is hanging down.

"That it is," Walter says. "I'll have to call someone."

"Let me see what I can quickly do with that gutter."

"No, that's alright," Walter says, "We'll call—"

Boon is already down the porch stairs. "It'll just take me second." He hops onto the air-conditioner vent. It whirs beneath him, makes his voice stumble.

He brings his fist up and with two hard pounds secures the gutter. He jumps down, brushing the dirt from his hands. He looks at Walter for some kind of approval. Walter gives him a quick nod of the head, and Boon returns it.

Then Boon walks up the driveway and grabs the swinging cord of the carport tarp and begins to retie the knot. "You're going to have to replace this fairly soon," Boon says of the tarp, "but it should hold." He goes on to tighten the other two cords.

"Yeah, I'll probably put up a new one soon."

Boon runs across the yard with his hands up like he's about to catch a pass. He barrels up the porch steps like he's going to say something, but pinches back a mischievous smile and drops his arms to his side.

He leans against the porch rail and says, "Wilvin told me to see you about the bonfire, said you were the best. I want to help."

"Okay, the guys show up Christmas Eve morning, early, five-ish. And we spend the day building. There's a whole crew of us, thirteen, fourteen. If you find any good wood between now and then, let me know."

"I was hoping to...I used to drive up from Morgan City every year. Drive along the whole stretch of fires. I've got access to wood."

"There's rules."

"So I've heard. I got a sister that works for the Tennessee Wildlife and Fishery. I've spent whole summers putting out wildfires. You know they take stuff down every day from disease, land clearing."

"Great, let me know what you find." Walter puts out his hand to shake, "It was nice to meet you."

"I see you've got some Alligator wood," Boon says, referring to the sweetgum branches, because of the way the bark attaches to the tree in plates edgewise rather than laterally.

"Good eye, but those branches don't dry out. They'll be rot by the twenty-fourth."

Boon walks across the lawn and picks up one of the branches, examines it. "Good wings," he says of the branches' ridges. "More surface area, good for burning. Where'd you store it?"

"The garage."

Boon shakes his head, "That's the problem. This wood is hardly ever used as an outdoor material because it rots so quickly."

Walter is impressed.

"You got a spare bedroom?"

"Yeah, in the attic."

"You just lay it down on some paper towels, not too thick, maybe even turn the heat up a little higher than usual for a couple of nights. Then season it like you would a log. Cut up in the bark some before you do." He puts a stack of the branches on the porch. Then he loads the rest in his truck for him to do. "It'll be dry, Boss. Trust me."

When Boon is done he shakes Walter's hand. "Nice to meet you," he says. "I'll see you on Wednesday."

"What's Wednesday?" Walter says.

"It's a surprise," Boon says and climbs into his truck.

Walter watches wet leaves stick to the tires of a passing car. While growing up it was Collins's job to mow the lawn and Walter's to sweep. As soon as Collins was done, he'd get the hose and let it loose on the yard. Wet grass is a pain in the ass.

Boon's truck roars down the street, sucking up large piles of leaves in its tires. Walter looks down at the pile of sweetgum branches.

Boon has put the first of the bonfire wood right in front of him.

Walter can't explain how he feels, how joy can resemble emotions one assumes to be its opposite.

He thinks of that night in 1968 when he and Collins were huddled on the back porch around an ancient Bakelite, listening to their hero Catfish Hunter pitch a perfect game against the Minnesota Twins. Catfish went three for five, drove in three of the game's four runs. Not one Twin touched first base. He was only twenty-two years old. "Catfish not caught, Catfish—" the broadcaster was trying to talk, an audible knot in his voice, "Today, folks—" but the collective swell of the crowd engulfed everything.

Walter hasn't thought about baseball in years. He still remembers the spring Collins busted his knee catching a game in college. There had been talk that he was good enough for the minors, maybe even more than that.

The knee never really healed, and Collins quit before the doctor told him he had to.

After that, baseball became a solemn thing in their house. It was a subject never mentioned by name. A channel changed faster than a Baptist broadcast service.

"The girls cancelled," Phoebe says. She's in the dining room, refolding the cloth napkins and putting them in the mahogany buffet.

Walter looks at the only remaining place setting and then at her.

"I ate a late lunch with Mom today," she says. She picks up a wine glass, thumbs at a stain, then places it gently in the china cabinet.

Walter sits in his place at the dining room table, and Phoebe brings him a warmed plate of lamb chops, greens and corn from the kitchen.

Without saying anything, she puts a stack of plates in the cabinet next to the silver chalices. Collins's daughter, Eleanor, used to ask to drink apple juice out of them during sleepovers.

"Not the fancy glasses," Phoebe would say and later to Walter, "Where does she get these ideas?"

"Who knows," Walter would say. But he was the one who used to sneak them juice in fancy glasses to toast during Phoebe and Walter's Christmas party.

Phoebe picks up the centerpiece from the table and fits it back on the mantel in between miniature paintings of faded saints with rotting frames and portraits of relatives, dead and living.

She fixes the dried-out palmetto fronds in a green ceramic vase. She picks up the unused silverware from the table. Some of the silver is her maternal grandmother's, some of it her paternal great-grandmother's.

Their house is an inescapable conversation with the past.

"Mom didn't remember how to use one," Phoebe says, holding up a spoon. "We sat down to eat this potato and vegetable mash with shredded meat that the doctor recommended. And she sat there and stared down at her plate for a long time. Then she took her hand and scooped it into her mouth."

Phoebe puts the spoon in the velvet-lined box that was her mother's. No dinner is ever served without at least one piece of that silver, just like her mother had done. "And I said to her, 'Mom, use your spoon. Like this,' and I picked it up to show her.

"She looked at me without the faintest bit of recognition. Blankness. Blank eyes, blank everything. Not a peaceful blankness, but not frightened. It was as if she didn't even know what she'd lost."

"I'm so sorry," Walter says. He puts his hand on top of hers. "What'd you do?"

Phoebe moves her hand away. "I let her use her hands. I let my mother eat with her hands in the middle of an entire dining hall."

She brings the salad and bread basket into the kitchen and when she returns says, "I think I'm going to go for a drive." She has her purse on her shoulder and her keys in hand. "I need to—I need to feel the windows down."

Walter wants the right thing to say. All that comes is a neutral, "Of course."

He listens to her car start and the tires roll over and crunch down on the seed pods that litter the driveway.

ALL CHRISTMAS EVE DAY, DAD would light kerosene-soaked cotton balls on fire, call them dying birds, and send them rolling down the levee. Some died out before they hit the bottom. Some picked up more speed and power. Despite what they became, one thing was certain: his action set into play a whole slew of reactions. The dying bird effect.

Sometimes it hit someone's ankle (it bites with a tooth not stinger). Sometimes it created a sense of hostility because someone felt it was directly aimed at them (Walter more often than Collins for sure). Regardless, it always got someone pissed off or upset or chewed out. Someone stormed off or got the silent treatment for the rest of the day. Events big or small, one person or many, it didn't discriminate. Name calling, fist fights, it was even rumored to have played a role in their cousin Suzette's divorce. All of this so some old man with severe pyromaniac tendencies could feel as if he controlled fire.

They may all have fallen under that description, technically, but Dad was the worst.

On Tuesday morning, Pierre, their cocker spaniel, is their dying bird. He vomits all down the front steps and into Walter's shoes. Walter has to go a different route to work to bring him to the vet. Because Pierre's nails punch holes in the leather car seats, Walter takes the truck. All this causes a great deal of yelling and cursing.

After leaving Pierre at the vet and driving down Coliseum Street, past Napoleon Avenue, Walter sees a house being landscaped. Not a little resodding or poinsettia planting, but full-on, front yard rebirth. Everything uprooted, ripped out.

Walter parks the car and gets out. He goes up to the gate. In the yard, men wearing bandanas around their heads and soiled gardening gloves pull plants and pass them until they reach a dumpster parked in the driveway. Brown, limp flowers and weeds doing a final death dance.

Walter notices in the corner of the yard a birch tree and goes up closer for a better look. The tree leans against the fence, its roots unearthed. Walter can't tell if there is something wrong with it. He steps closer, almost into the bushes.

A birch tree. The paper tree. It's been used since prehistoric times. The bark is strong and water-resistant, yet it can be cut or bent. Medicinal, chemical, fungicidal. It's a preserver. A warrior against time and weather.

He climbs out of the bushes and walks toward the gate's entrance. "Excuse me," he says to any one of the men.

None of them notice. They continue with the digging and pulling and breaking of thick, stubborn roots. From an open car door in the driveway, a rap song carries their beat.

"Hey," he yells.

One of the men who's leaning over a barrel of fresh soil says, "Whaddya want?"

"What are you doing with that birch tree?"

"Don't know."

"Can I have it?"

"No."

Walter can't offer money or anything, so he doesn't have much leverage. "Do you know what's going to happen to it?"

"Look man, we've got a lot of work to do. We've been instructed to put everything we pull into that dumpster. Where it goes after that, I don't care."

"Can I scrape the bark from it before you put it in?"

"Man—"

"It'll take a second. It won't kill it, won't even damage it." He then adds an almost boyish, "Please."

"If it means you will leave, fine. Do it over there." He motions for one of the men to move the tree to the side of the dumpster.

It's Walter's for the picking. He lets himself in the gate and asks the one who brought it over for a trash bag. He gets up close, admires it.

White armor with specks of black. To render birch bark useless, it has to be soaked for a long time. That is how resilient it is.

He borrows a garden pick and cuts a slit length-wise through the bark. He gets a good grip with his hands and pries it away from the wood. It isn't the best quality bark. That would have come in spring, early summer. But it comes off easily enough. In large, thin sheets, he separates the outer layer from the trunk.

When the trash bag is almost full, Walter stands in the stranger's yard and holds up a sheath.

This here is my paper, he thinks, shamelessly, to mark for record the year I finally destroy Collins Doucet.

It is my paper, rolled and lit.

In the art of bonfire building, it is this type of dry wood material that readily catches a spark.

Walter has found his tinder.

When he gets in the car the first thing he wants to do is call Boon. Barely even knows the kid, but if he had his number he'd already be dialing it.

"We're on fire," he wants to say.

The excitement in him feels almost violent. "We're on fire."

Walter flies through his morning paperwork. He can't stop thinking about the bag of birch in the back of his truck. He finishes another chart and victoriously slaps it down on the completed pile. He flips open the next file and begins to scan glucose test results for a forty-three year old female patient. He thinks of taking an early lunch. He feels lucky today, wants to drive around and see what else is for the taking.

He thinks of '92 when Dad and Collins built a replica of the Civil War's Old Arsenal in Baton Rouge. It wasn't a very complicated structure, but it burned for a long time. Nine and a half hours. It was the year that he and Wilvin built a canon, a very square canon. Two and three-quarters hours.

"—Jesum," Walter looks up and Collins is standing in his office doorway. "What are you doing here?"

"I've been standing here for like fifteen minutes. Is it time for a hearing aid?"

"How the hell did you get in here?"

"Seems the nurses out front want a little bit of the C-Dawg."

"Don't call yourself that."

Collins sits back in the leather chair facing Walter's desk. He crosses his hands behind his head and looks around the office. He nods his head in approval. Nothing's changed since the last time he was here.

"It looks good," he says.

"Thanks." Walter says, but he's thinking of how his victory might wipe that smirk off his face.

"Wanna grab Bud's for lunch?"

"Are you not working today?"

"I'm in between appointments."

"I've got work."

"You don't get lunch?"

"Not today."

Collins takes a peppermint from the jar on Walter's desk. He unwraps it, pops it in his mouth and chews it. He takes another.

Walter's annoyance follows some rule of osmosis, filters towards the same thing every time. Collins.

"Can you not," Walter says as Collins reaches for two more, "eat all of them."

"I'm starving." He slumps in the chair, crosses his leg and rests his chin in his hand. "Sorry I interrupted your...zone."

Walter moves around papers like he's busy. Collins watches. He taps his foot against the chair.

"You're putting marks on my furniture."

"Wilvin's out."

"Impossible."

"Spoke with him last night. Says without his brother he's got nothing to compete for."

"Why would he tell you before he tells his own crew?"

"Think he was hoping that I'd tell you."

The order of command. Phone calls, laundry folding, dishwashing. Growing up, things were delegated among Dad, Collins and Walter by rank, which was determined by age. Wilvin, being the oldest, trumped them all.

"He's still going to be around, just not taking sides," Collins says. He picks up a paperweight from Walter's desk and pretends to drop it. "You pissed?"

"No," Walter bluffs. He focuses on straightening the files in front of him.

Wilvin J. Doucet, III. Uncle Willy. He married Esman Bigler, Big Essie, when he was seventeen and she fifteen. They lived in the same house in Gramercy for fifty-three years before he lost her eight years ago to a freak infection after routine knee surgery.

Before retiring, Uncle Wilvin worked for the electric company for forty-seven years. If the bonfire was a display of lights, he and Walter would be unbeatable.

Wilvin could make a lightbulb work with the blind components of a woman's purse. He'd have the entire structure strung up to some main power line three parishes over and shining bright as the sun for days.

When Walter was fourteen, he watched Wilvin wrap a board in Christmas lights before lighting it. Walter covered his ears, waited for the explosion. Instead there were a few small pops, nothing more than a flick of sound, before it all melted into each other. Fire is a far cry from electricity.

Wilvin could also draw exactly any municipal building or maritime structure there was. But when it came to building it, he was not so great. Not like his brother, Hyde. He found decent wood. But understanding the physics behind the rates of oxidizing wood, depending on shape, age, and moisture? Forget about it.

"—Visualization. That's what it is," Collins is saying. He's taken another peppermint. "I could see the last shot before I sunk it. You know, see it before it was there."

It dawns on Walter what Wilvin stepping down means.

This is the first time it's only Walter against Collins. This can be the only year that ever matters. The year that ends it all.

There can be a final victor.

"I have to be in surgery," Walter lies.

"Yes then, doctor, I'll leave you be." Collins gets up, slightly genuflects in front of the desk.

As Collins leaves the office, he slaps the top frame of the door. Something he's always done, but it fills Walter with an unexplainable anger.

He wants to see a look of defeat on Collins's face. He, and only he, wants to be the one to put it there. He knows the face he's going for. It needs to be similar to how he looked when the Air Force rejected him on the basis of a low-functioning left ear from a ruptured eardrum that never fully healed. His balance is off.

"In more ways than one," Walter had joked at the time.

Walter wants to be the news that Collins will never fly an F-14 or a Cobra or test human acceleration. And he wants to be the one to deliver it.

Walter pauses in his backyard and inhales the chilly air. It's smoky and rich. A house nearby has lit a fire. It smells like they've used a pre-dipped log, maybe maple.

The first fire Walter ever built was on a hunting trip with Dad and Collins. He couldn't have been older than ten. He wasn't able to light it with just matches so Dad splashed it with lighter fluid. He dropped four slices of bacon and a piece of sausage in the fire trying to cook and keep it lit at the same time.

In the garage, Walter plugs in his table saw. He pulls down a pair of plastic goggles from a crooked nail. All along the back wall are rusted bikes, deflated balls, lost screws, solo shoes. The beginnings of a tree house. An almost finished bird house. He'd tried to teach Claudine how to saw.

"Can I throw it out?" he recently asked Claudine. "Or will you take what you want to your own garage?"

"Just keep it, Dad," she said. "For now." And so he does.

Walter tears back the plastic sheath over his wood crib. Tut returned a pile of wood that Walter gave him after last year. They're downed branches from Audubon Park that Walter had found.

Live oak. Seasoned for over a year now. It doesn't get much better than that.

Oak is a hardwood. It's one of the hardest, heaviest woods there is. The frame of the USS Constitution (replicated for a Doucet fire in 1963) was built of live oak. The wood's density was what protected the ship against heavy artillery fire.

Its heating value increases the longer it's been seasoned. It's easy to split, few sparks, slight fragrance, moderately easy to start, light smoke (unseasoned smokes more), and excellent coaling qualities.

Walter is going to mix some of these older branches with newer ones to make the crown for the pyre.

He guides the first branch towards the rolling blade.

The grinding saw is the Doucet men's language. A moment of grief over their mother. A failing report card. Ways to avoid getting a girl pregnant. Talk came around the saw. Their words, stiff jolts between hollowed-out vibrations.

Walter admires the white, brittle insides of the branch. A crack runs through the piece with lots of little cracks along the inner rings. There is a muscular delicacy to even the hardest of woods.

Every time the blade hits the wood, Walter feels a surge of energy.

The weight of the world is shredded in that sound. It gives hope to something at the end of it, something on the other side of it. He is always almost there.

He cuts small grooves in the branches so that they fit down into each other.

He makes a pile of leaves and small twigs he pulls. He thinks of the word "strill." He and Collins invented it when they were boys, warriors, to determine why one and not the other built their fort in the best spot, rescued the princess, won the battle, enjoyed the feast. Victory was determined by the strength of one's will. Twigs and leaves. From the small, the mighty rise.

Walter's calloused hands bring down the saw on another branch. They are covered in scars from small nicks over time. He has never been afraid to risk his surgeon hands for the cut of the saw. He stops to wipe the layer of sawdust that's collected around his mouth and nose.

"Boss?" Boon says as he walks up the driveway. "You feel like taking a drive?"

"Look how clean these grooves are," Walter says. He holds out a branch. Sawdust clings to his forearms, shirt, neck.

Boon inspects his work. "Nice."

Tied in the bed of Boon's truck is a large, barking Catahoula.

"Lie down, Chief," Boon says, and climbs in. "It's out off Airline Highway." He starts the engine.

"What is?"

"Surprise."

In the car, a low-voiced woman croons about waiting for people to leave love.

Boon's choice of music is unexpected. Walter tries not to smile.

"I like the beard you got working there," Walter says. "Makes you look more, more—"

"—It's OK, Boss. I'll probably shave it tonight."

They talk a few minutes about Wilvin, a little bit about the wood they still need to get.

Mainly, the focus is on Alma. Boon wants to know what she was like as a girl. If it's true that she shot her first deer at nine? Yes. If she really has never eaten mustard? Don't know. Was her hair always as curly? Her eyes always as green?

"Ask her."

"She says, 'women need their secrets.'"

"They tend to have a lot of those."

They drive down Airline Highway towards the airport. "Just you wait, you're gonna love this place," Boon says.

They pass a nameless motel. The Escape Lounge advertises 'BBQ-n-Buckets.' There's an old billboard for a gun show from the previous year, an emptied Zephyr Car Wash, a drive-thru Daiquiris, Ace Cash Express, a place to rent Porta Potties. It's the land of misplaced dreams.

Walter thinks of the year of the tallest towers. His crew's Chrysler building was one of their best. One of his cousins at the time was dating a man who carved detail into the wood. It was beautiful.

Dad and Collins won with their Empire State building that looked no different than the Washington Monument. It was taller, but only by a Louisiana flag they stuck from the pyre. If only Walter's crew had had a damn flag, any flag.

This was before height restrictions were capped at twenty feet after a collapse killed two men in Convent.

"Can I ask you something, Boss?"

"Sure."

"What is it that women really want?"

"How the hell do I know?"

"You've had a good-looking wife for the past thirty years."

"Thanks?"

"What's the secret? Is it like something you do or say?"

"I don't know of any secrets."

"Is it a sex thing? 'Cause I've got this buddy of mine who said if you—"

"What? Get out of here. We aren't having this conversation."

On the radio, a woman laments becoming lost in someone's head.

Walter wants to say something proverbial. Something about a man finding something in him that he didn't know existed. How love is realizing someone else put it there. "I don't have anything for you. Maybe, go after what you want?"

"I could use something a little more concrete than that," Boon says. "Are you sure you don't get her on her stomach—"

"—Done. Pull over."

"I'm joking. I'm joking."

Walter shakes his head and looks out the window to hide his smile.

He watches as a cloud passes in front of the sun and in an instant, it seems like rain. The cloud's edges glow from the sun before it releases the light again.

There's Lions Bingo Hall and the Jefferson Flea Market with outdated washing machines and broken baby cradles in the parking lot. The Mud Hole. A Wagner's Meat Market is also a gas station.

They pass Able Body Labor with a parked Silverado painted as an American flag. A large eagle is sprayed on the side of the bed. Their augur. What's to come worries Walter.

They pass the airport and eventually pull into a gutted-looking warehouse.

"What's this?" Walter says.

"A graveyard of sorts," Boon says. He makes the sign of the cross, kisses two fingers and taps the roof above him.

Boon jumps out as a skinny man walks towards them, wiping his hands on a dirtied cloth.

"What's up, Fryhead," the man says.

Boon clasps the man's hand in both of his, gives him a good shake.

Inside the warehouse are endless stacks of doors, frames, mantels, banisters, hutches. Molding of all kinds. Woodwork, emptied from homes, comes here to be resold to people renovating old New Orleans houses. It's a necropolis, where the bones keep getting dug up.

"Whaddya got for us?" Boon says.

"The stack over here," the man says, ushering them to a back corner. "None of it can be salvaged."

There's a door frame the size of a wall. The wood splits all along the edges. A stack of thick oak and cypress doors with large cracks down the middle and handles missing. Smaller door frames lean against each other. They are old and chipped and missing chunks of molding.

Light rakes along the wood, then is gone. Walter looks up to find a large hole in the roof of the warehouse. The light returns, finding its way through rafters covered with roosting pigeons and birdshit. It brings forth an inrush of power.

"It's yours for the picking," the man says.

"We're gonna take it all right off your hands, podna," Boon says. Walter can hear the excitement in his voice. They can see their fire through worn out pantry and bathroom doors.

"I got a shredder out back too," the man says. "Isn't that what you said you needed?"

"Right, Boss?" Boon turns to Walter.

"Yeah, shred about three quarters of it," Walter says. "The rest, we'll chop."

"You got it," the man says. He calls a guy over to help him move it out back.

Walter pats Boon on the shoulder.

A secret in bonfire building is that the pyre is never powerful enough to rise alone. It needs guts. Scrap lumber, broken pallets, shavings, sticks fill the inside of the pyre. Oak and cypress are about as strong as it gets.

"You son of—come here," Walter wraps his arms partly around Boon's big shoulders and hugs him. "I can't believe this."

"Sure thing, Boss."

The man comes back and gives them both a pair of gloves so they can help haul. Boon and Walter bring some of the pieces they don't want shredded to the truck.

Then they stand out back and watch as the men break up the wood with axes and slide it into the shredder. Small pieces shoot out into large burlap sacks.

They are the Natchez preparing for the Feast of New Fire, kindling oak bark on an altar to relight the houses of an entire village.

Oak will hallow their fire.

Walter and Phoebe's attic is packed to the brim, and there hasn't been a working light up there for years. It is so dark you can't see past your hand. Walter grabs a book of matches on his way up. He strikes one at the top of the stairs. The flame throws shadows of old toys, records, clothes and furniture on the wall. Proof that something existed before it's gone. The match burns out.

Walter goes to strike another but it breaks. The last one, and it breaks too. In the darkness, he carefully climbs the rest of the shaky stairs and fumbles around for where he thinks the box of lights is. He opens one box and feels around. Ski equipment. Another is old shoes. Finally, he finds the wheels and wheels of plastic bulbs and he knows the box is labeled in Phoebe's handwriting, Lights.

"Sure you don't mind?" Walter asks as he hands down the box to Boon.

"Not at all, Boss."

On the front lawn, Walter and Boon unravel the lights, decide which strings will go where. When Claudine was ten or eleven, Walter asked her to help. He thought it could be their thing. She'd barely gotten one strand of lights spread out on the lawn before saying, "This is impossible. Call me when they're pretty."

"It's been a while since I've done this," Boon says.

"You don't hang lights?"

"I'm not really from a big Christmas family. I offered to hang lights for Alma. Set up a tree. She said it was something she did with her mom. I get it. I was raised by a single mom. We have our things we do just the two of us. Not holiday stuff but…you know."

"Has your family met Alma?" Walter asks.

"It's more like has Alma met the family. No. Not in its entirety. My mom has and my two younger brothers."

"What'd they think? Did she pass the test?" Walter jokes.

"My mom thought she seemed nice. Liked how she did her nails. One of my brothers thought her hair was too big. It's just curly, you know, makes it look bigger."

Working from the left side of the house to the right, Walter and Boon slowly circle each porch column, drape each bush and banister.

"What was her dad like?" Boon asks.

"Nobody really knew him. He wasn't around for that long, one bonfire, maybe two."

"Alma said he helped build the Egyptian pyramid bonfire."

"Could have. Don't really remember."

"I think my dad built the roof of my mom's house. That's what she says."

Walter gets out the ladder and wraps the lower branches of the sweetgum. Phoebe's car pulls up the driveway as he's rounding the trunk.

"Walter, this is going to be wonderful," she says with a youthful bounce. "It looks like you've hung so many. It's just perfect." She walks up and hugs him from behind. It surprises him when she greets him with a kiss.

"How was your day?" he asks.

"Someone put a contract in for the listing over on Willow." Another kiss. "It makes me think of Celebration in the Oaks," Phoebe says of the lights, the whimsy in her voice building. In City Park each year, two million lights decorate the hundred-year-old trees.

"Who was in the car with us that year Jolie got sick on chocolate?"

Walter says. It makes Phoebe laugh. "Was it Alma? Was Alma with us that year?"

"I don't think so," Phoebe says. "Maybe, but I think it was some of Claudine's school friends." She leans on Walter's shoulder like she used to. "It's really something, Walter. It never gets old."

"Ready, Boss," Boon says from the porch. He's hooked the lights up to two extension cords.

"I give you light," Walter says as Boon plugs it in.

The universe has unzipped her dress, draped it over their house. It is covered in stars from a sky on a moonless night.

"Merry Christmas," Phoebe says. "Y'all want some hot chocolate?"

"I'd love some," Boon says.

"Call the girls," Walter says, "Call the girls and tell them to come over."

There is only a small flicker before half the lights fall dead. Patterns of random dark patches appear. The house is asymmetrical. Parts of it have vanished. It is lopsided, falling with only one column. The banisters aren't rooted into the porch. The tree has just the top half of a trunk, branches grow only on the right side.

Phoebe steps back. "It doesn't even make sense which ones went out."

"Is it the socket?" Walter says. Boon fiddles with it. No.

"Did you test them?" Phoebe says.

"You saw them, they worked," Walter says.

"We can't leave it like this. It looks awful. They're going to have to come down." Phoebe opens the trunk of her car and gets out her briefcase.

Walter looks at the ground. There's enough light to have her shadow stretch up the driveway and reach him. He watches it circle him as she crosses the lawn towards the front door.

That is where joy lives, Walter thinks, in the space between darkness and knowing.

ONE THURSDAY EVERY MONTH, THE hospital smells of old man's aftershave. It's something they clean the floors with, but it makes Walter think of his mentor, Dr. Mehra. He can still see the small man with his arms elbow-deep in a patient's cavity instructing Walter that outside of Western medicine, the kidneys are linked emotionally to determination and willpower.

Like an infomercial, Walter recites Dr. Mehra's list. The kidneys don't just filter the body's blood. They regulate blood pressure, stimulate bone marrow, monitor oxygen.

They're responsible for the functioning of the ears, the opening and closing of the bladder and anus, the production of brain matter. They support memory.

"What do we have?" Walter says as he pushes through the ER doors.

A resident follows close behind, "Female, white, 65. Came in complaining of lower back pain. Itching on hands. BUN and creatinine levels are elevated. Two years in remission. She's requested you."

Walter orders more tests to be done, urine and blood cells. He opens the drape to find a woman lying on the gurney close to tears.

"Mrs. Powers," Walter says. He recognizes her.

"Dr. Doucet, I'm glad I got you."

"We are just going to have a quick look here." Walter presses down on her abdomen. "Pain? Tender?"

"No."

He has her lie on her stomach as the nurse squirts a gel on her lower back. Using an ultrasound machine, Walter checks for any obstruction in the kidneys. "They look clear. You know the drill."

She grabs onto the sheet and exhales while Walter plunges a thin needle through the skin and into each kidney. He draws out bits of tissue and sends them to the lab to biopsy.

"We'll be in touch," Walter says and pats her on the hand. He orders fluids and drugs to make her comfortable.

Walter tries to remember what Dr. Mehra told him about the Ancient Egyptians. They left the kidneys outside of a mummified corpse or something like that, in order to be judged.

"Male, white, 52. History of renal impairment. Signs of resistant edema," a resident says to Walter as they walk to the next examination room.

Walter opens the door to find a man with his eyes almost swollen shut. His legs, ankles, wrists thick with a purplish hue.

"What do we do?" Walter quizzes the resident.

"Furosemide?"

"How much?"

"40 mg bolus IV and bumetanide 2 mg IV."

"This should remove the excess fluid," Walter says to the patient. Saying this makes Walter think of how an unseasoned live oak can carry as much as 330 gallons of water.

Walter tells the resident to page him when this is done and heads towards his office.

As he walks toward the end of the hall, he hears a recorded voice coming from one of the offices. It's Dr. Erickson's. The door is ajar, but the room is empty.

On the desk is a small radio delivering a religious broadcast. The voice is low and cracked but authoritative. The language moves between maybe West African and an English translator, "In whom we have redemption, through his blood, according to the richness of his grace. He can undo your curdling tide once your soul is offered."

The Greek word for kidney is nephros, translated as kidney (plural), an uncertain affinity, or more figuratively, the inmost mind, the reins.

In wasn't until recent editions that the Bible substituted the word reins for soul or mind.

"Let the Lord wake your mind," the voice commands.

It makes Walter think of Uncle Bam, who wasn't really his uncle, and his late night preaching around a camp fire. Except his was never about God, it was about baseball and women's ankles. That was his religion. Never have a player's stats been more passionately delivered alongside an elegy of an ex-wife's lower legs.

On the desk next to the radio and a dashboard hula girl is a hippopotamus tchotchke holding a sign: Inter urinas et faeces nascimur. Erickson jokes it's his dirty for the nerdy.

Walter shuts the door and goes to his office. He sits at his desk and without thinking, opens the bottom drawer. He pulls out the copy of Dad's file.

He scans over the test results he's seen many times. He looks for a new pattern to emerge. Something he's missed.

BUN and creatinine levels. Aggregations of red and white blood cells. Levels of magnesium, sodium, potassium, phosphorus. Proteins in urine.

Lesions of the intrarenal vasculature. Toxic acute tubular necrosis. Interstitial nephritis. Myeloma casts.

He wants a clue, an over-looked relationship.

Glomerular filtration rate. Albuminuria. Nothing is connecting.

Walter closes the file, locks it back in the drawer. He wonders if what Dr. Mehra use to say is true. In Eastern medicine, it's thought that the water element of the kidneys nourishes the wood element of the liver. The unison of the two ensures regeneration, flowing and releasing.

They make sure fires don't accumulate in the body.

B Y SATURDAY, DECEMBER 10TH, TUT's brother has gotten his hands on some beech wood, a decent hardwood. And a buddy of his thinks he's found some seasoned cypress. Though neither of them have been very reliable sources in the past. Walter's cousin, Shane, thinks he may have some fir. Some hardwood, some softwood.

Walter is spending the weekend with the men at Boon's hunting camp on a bayou outside of Morgan City. Around four in the afternoon, he arrives at the lot Boon told him about. He unloads his gear and waits. Water stretches all around him. The sun, low in the sky, lights the trees lining the banks. It hits the water, then jumps off.

In the lot, a flock of gulls fights over a fish carcass.

Twelve-year-old Walter freezes from the waist-high, marsh water behind his grandparents' house. His socks are wet and he stumbles in over-sized, mallard green galoshes. He tries to wade behind his brother, Dad in the lead with a rifle. Walter is their Labrador, dragging a limp bag in his teeth. When his feet struggle to grip the mud and his head falls under and he can taste the metal of blood on his lips, he gets hushed. Too young, too weak. Atta boy.

Walter hears the engine of a motorboat spit along the water. He sees Boon, standing up in the flatboat as he steers, with one hand flashing a few mini-salutes.

"Ahoy," Walter says.

"Hope you weren't waiting long?" Boon says. They load the boat and set off towards a canopy of bending trees. Slowly they ride, as if entering an empty cathedral or ancient ruin. They follow the narrow canal with tall trees like columns on either side. Moss, collected dust.

It's a sanctuary for the nearly dead or newly born.

The vaulted way opens up to green-coated water and grassy patches of reeds. The marsh is a sprawl of bald cypresses with scorched tops and unsettled roots.

A white egret fishes.

Civilization dissolves.

They come to a half-sunk dock and a path that leads up to a rustic cabin on stilts. Most of the screens are busted on the windows. The door is tied shut with an electrical cord. The refrigerator is the cooler sitting on the porch. The only sink, a simple bucket and spigot next to three coffee cans of bacon grease.

"Wilvin got here last night. So did some of my buddies. Your brother, this morning. I think y'all are going to like it," Boon says as they dock the boat. He ties the rope to the post and attaches a bell, "Alarm system."

Walter steps into the soft mud. He hasn't been hunting in a long time. The bayou smells sweet and dank like gym shoes or flowers Phoebe has left out too long.

There's a sign over the front door that says Where Y'at? The inside of the cabin is one room. Beds line the walls, a few bunk beds. Sleeping bags and duffles claim some of them. The walls are uninsulated wood.

Sprawled out on the bottom bunk of a bed under a small window is Collins, waking from a nap in his clothes.

"What do you think of my new boots?" Collins has on new nylon wading shoes Walter has seen in a magazine: khaki color, tough canvas, dual heel and toe traction.

"I think you're going to get them dirty."

Walter looks out the window. The sun is leaving the sky a raw red.

The river, in search of a steeper, more direct route to the Gulf, shifts its delta mouth. The abandoned courses become bayous, pockets where the water runs still.

"Anybody get anything yet?" Walter says.

"Not that I know of."

Collins's nervous reflex is sex jokes. He's done it since they were in high school. And as soon as the men gather around the fire, filling paper plates with red beans and rice and some of Boon's boudin, he begins.

"What do hurricanes and women have in common?" he says. He stands clipping the rim of a red plastic cup with his fingers and trying to balance a full plate.

Most of the men are focused on the food. They eat quickly with their heads down.

"What?" Walter finally says.

"They're wet, unpredictable furies that take your car and house when they leave."

There's a few laughs.

Boon stands over the fire, stirring the pot. The ground is so wet that the fire is made in a metal cylinder. On a few spokes he has some tough-looking pieces of sausage.

The men don't say much as they eat. There's only the sound of forks scraping plates.

"A husband and wife are in the shower," Collins says. He's already starting to laugh himself. "And the doorbell rings."

Walter watches the faces of the men. They seem interested.

"So the wife goes to the front door in her robe, and the husband's friend is there and he says 'I'll give you two hundred dollars to open your robe.' When she gets back to the bathroom, the husband asks who it was. The wife tells him and he says, 'that SOB owes me two hundred dollars.'"

More laughs this time.

"Good one," Boon's cousin says.

"Give it a rest," Wilvin says.

"I got a story for ya," Boon says.

Collins sits down on one of the logs surrounding the fire pit and eats.

Boon cuts up the pieces of sausage and passes them around.

"This gator," he says and holds up a piece of the meat. "True story about this gator. My buddy—"

"Who?" pipes his friend.

"John Gatreaux."

"Ah, good guy."

"We'd just gotten the gator to take the bait and we're waiting for the perfect shot. And it's thrashing around when John loses his balance and falls in. I heard a smack as he went in, his head against the boat. The line's twisting and fraying. I'm screaming his name at the few bubbles that are coming up where he went under. When all of a sudden everything goes still. I can't waste any time so I yank the line as hard as

I can and fire a shot. It misses, ricochets off the side of the boat. Some of it lodges in my forearm." Boon points to the scar.

The men are hanging on to every word.

"I fire again. Bulls-eye. The gator goes limp on the line. I don't even think I just jump in the water, feeling around for my buddy. Pull him up by the hair. There's still bait in the water so we have to get out of there quick. I hoist him in the boat, start giving him CPR. He's blue. I think he's dead until he finally starts coughing. I smack him on the back a few times.

"Keep in mind, we still got a three hundred pound dead gator on the line that's not going to hold forever. And he sits up and he says, 'Death doesn't come after life it comes before. We've got it backwards.'"

Some of the men laugh at this.

"I said, 'See what comes after this, Einstein,' and tried to push him back in."

"Crazy guy," one of the men says. The men laugh.

Walter thinks about the last time he shot a deer, maybe he was sixteen. Dad hung it up by the hind legs. They wiped blood on his face. He was given a knife and a jar to collect the piss. When Walter gutted the sandy-colored, swollen carcass, a pink-filled placenta, slimed with purple and blue streaks emptied to the ground with the blood and intestines.

"Goddamit, boy," Dad said. "You don't shoot the women."

Boon tosses some more wood into the fire pit. Sparks spray. Light pulses against the dying day, crawls over logs and disappears into the trees. The men's faces are occasionally lit, then wiped away by rotating shadows.

They all stare into the fire, waiting for it to reveal something.

"I hear you boys can build a hell of a fire," one of Boon's buddies says to Wilvin and Walter and Collins.

"We try," Wilvin says.

"What's the secret?" another one asks.

"I'd dose it in so much gasoline," a third one says.

"There isn't just one thing," Wilvin says.

"I'd burn a mattress," the third one says. "Those shits don't even burn."

Collins gets up and throws his plate in the trash can. He heads to the cabin and comes back with his hunting gear.

Walter gets up and goes over to him. Boon does too.

"Where you going?" Walter asks.

"Night hunt," Collins says.

"Right now?" Walter asks.

"Head west, not north," Boon says.

"Got it," Collins says. "Was it you or Dad that taught us how to survive coyotes?" Collins says to Wilvin.

"Not me," Wilvin says.

"I don't think it's coyotes you have to be worried about out here, Boss," Boon says.

"No, I know," Collins says. "I was just," he walks off towards the trees. Walter watches until he's swallowed by blackness. He listens to his footsteps drag along the ground, kicking stones and snapping sticks.

Walter follows after him. "Collins, wait."

"What?" Collins snaps on his flashlight and shines it directly into Walter's eyes.

Walter shields his face. "Everything okay?"

"Fine." Collins walks off into the woods. Walter watches the small trail of light before it's extinguished by the night.

"'...We just built a new stadium in less than six months, twice the size too,' the Texan says to the Cajun." One of the guys is telling a joke. "'Same with a new bridge. How long did it take you to build that bridge?' The Texan points to the Mississippi Bridge.

"And the Cajun says, 'I don't know, but it wasn't there this morning.'"

Walter sits back down by the fire. He waits for the bottle of Wild Turkey to make its way to him.

The fire howls to the sky. It is a rabid beast, waiting for them to avert their eyes. If unleashed, it will devour any living thing. And if contained, it will eventually consume itself in a final, cannibalistic act.

They don't hear Collins coming. There's the crackle hiss of the fire. Another story about gators. And then Collins steps into the light with his gun slung over his shoulder.

"Back so soon?" someone says.

Collins slips the gun sling over his head and puts his rifle down on the ground. "It's scary as shit out there," he says.

The men laugh.

"I hear that," one of them says. "You couldn't pay me to hunt out there this late."

Collins pours himself some Wild Turkey. "I got one more for tonight," he says and doesn't sit down. "A police officer gets off duty early. It was a rough shift and he's exhausted. It's two in the morning when he gets home and he doesn't want to wake his wife. So he quietly takes off his clothes and is about to carefully climb into bed when his wife says she needs aspirin and they're out. She has a horrible headache. 'Of course,' he says and feels his way around the dark room to get dressed. He half-asleep makes his way to the corner drugstore and the cashier says, "I know you. You're Officer Brown, right?'

'I am,' he says.

'Then why are you dressed up like the Fire Chief?'"

"I don't get it," one of the men says.

"It's not his clothes." Collins forces a smile. "Get it? There's another man."

It's too late. The joke is sunk.

Collins drains his cup. "'Night, gentlemen," he says with false confidence and finds his way to the cabin.

It makes Walter think of him bragging years ago, "Five times a week, at least."

Walter couldn't tell if Collins was lying, so he said, "Isn't it for most?" Walter wasn't even close.

Now, he's lucky if he gets that in a year.

The men burrow into their jackets. The fire is dying down.

Walter thinks of how wood, when burned, goes through three stages. In the first, wood is heated until the moisture within the wood cells can evaporate. In the second, the dried wood undergoes a chemical breakdown. The volatile gasses and liquids burn. This produces the flame. The final stage occurs when the charcoals burn and the embers glow. It's always in this order, though not all woods progress the same.

Walter feels the chill, blackness of night on his back, ready to pull him away from the fire any chance it gets.

Heat is ever-dispersing. It flows from hot to cold.

They are moving towards cool, still swamp mud.

"I T's TIME," A HUSKY VOICE says in the darkness of the cabin. It's the middle of the night when Walter gets a whiff of coffee and onion breath.

"What? No," he says and pulls the sleeping bag up over his head.

"Boss," a hand shakes him, "Boss, wake up."

Walter sits up. "What do you want, Boon?"

"We got some hogs to get. Need your help."

Walter unzips his bag and a cold stream of air slides up his boxers. "Godammit," he says.

Boon waits outside the door while Walter gets dressed. A thin, gray-blue line of light squints through the crack of the door.

Walter looks at Collins sleeping, at his mouth opening and closing in a familiar slant. The left side of his lower lip droops. Walter is not sure if he's ever seen his brother's adult face sleep before, but it looks just like it did when he was a kid.

"Shut the fuck up, will you?" Collins mutters and rolls over.

Last night's fire still smokes. Two of Boon's cousins sleep in bags right up against the pit's rocks. Puffs of Walter's breath take shape in the cool, damp air. A silence permeates the camp, except for the occasional rip of a bird's caw.

Walter finds Boon wrapping gear in waterproof tarp and tying it down in a flat-bottomed, fan boat.

"There's a good place about a half mile upstream," Boon says and points to a pair of high-waders for Walter to put on. He has a gun slung over his shoulder.

"Don't I need a gun?" Walter asks. He slides on the plastic overalls and climbs into the boat.

"Nah, we're just checkin' on some traps."

A dense fog spills out over the morning. In dim light, the bayou plays tricks on the eyes. Things move, disappear, reappear larger. The landscape of the day refuses to keep a solid form. The trees bend down, stand straight again. An unseen bird screams. Moss shines like the end of a snare.

The backwaters beckon, dare them to enter.

Boon hands Walter a canteen of sweetened chicory coffee, and before long they're skidding at what feels like 60 miles an hour with white wash chasing behind them.

"You ever hunt hogs?" Boon yells over the noise of the boat. His cheeks push in and back from the force of the wind and the speed.

Walter feels his lips flap. "First time," he yells back.

Boon slows down the boat as they reach an area of heavy marsh with high, thick grasses. "You don't wanna suck that stuff into the propeller, trust me." He maneuvers the boat on water so shallow that Walter can see mud at arm's reach.

"There are a few ways to hunt hog," Boon says. "One is you can wait in a stand and hope they're passing towards a good food source. Another is you can track them with dogs. My Chief isn't much of a hunter. Third way is with traps. I've found this to be the best."

Once they reach land, the sun is already breaking the blue-ish, silver wash of morning.

They get out and wade in the water, pulling the boat onto the bank. They tie it to a tree with roots that bend so much, the thing looks like it's kneeling in the mud.

The ground gets drier as they walk inland. They come to a shed that Boon unlocks. They put most of their gear in there and take off their waders.

Boon opens the other side of the shed and drags out two four-wheelers.

"I've got a three-inch scar on my left knee from one of these," Walter says.

"Climb on, Boss."

Boon revs the engine and rides off. Walter follows.

They come to a primitive-looking wood-framed cage with metal-mesh casing, rectangular in shape, one end panel tied in and up and ready to be triggered. The first trap is empty.

"The traps don't kill them?" Walter asks.

"What? Nah."

"Who kills them?"

"We do." Boon fiddles with the frame some.

"What's that smell?" Walter asks. It has a nauseating affect, like syrup and car exhaust.

"They like to roll around in molasses and diesel." Boon gets out a canister to freshen the bait.

"What's in that?" Walter asks.

"They like corn, stuff high in fat, and sweet stuff." Boon fits the canister back into his pack. "I use Jell-O powder. Don't go telling everybody now."

"Secret's safe," Walter says and crosses his heart.

"How many bullets before they go down?" Walter asks when they get back on the four-wheelers.

Boon doesn't hear him, drives on.

The brush around them becomes thicker. Bristles catch Walter's legs as he rides through. Up ahead, Walter hears a high-pitched whine followed by low groaning. He wishes he had a gun.

They stop in a small patch of open land. A trapped, wild hog snorts and thrashes its legs.

The closer they get, the more wild it moves. It's about the size of two dogs, only lower to the ground, thicker. It has a big snout with tusks curled around the side of it. The hair on its back stands straight up. The hog whines and thrashes. The cage begins to move with it.

Walter steps back. "Shoot it," he says without thinking.

Boon tries to hand him a knife.

Walter shakes his head, "No thanks."

"Take it. Cut it right along the throat. Right here," Boon says, motioning towards his own neck.

Walter leans down and makes sure the hog is a male before taking the knife. He steps up to the cage and the hog goes wild.

"Wait," Boon says. "Wait." They stand there until it calms down. Boon tosses in some bait. "Now," he says when the hog bends to eat it.

When Walter shot a deer or caught a fish, death was at a distance. The moment of impact was measured by the pop of a rifle or the tug of a pole.

He expects the cut of the skin to be tough, the hog to fight. But the knife slides easily over the throat. The vein effortlessly opens up. The hog quickly falls still. And a thin line of blood trails away from it. Life drains without any knowing pause. There is no moment of impact.

"That's how it's done," Boon says.

They open the trap door and drag out the hog. They hoist it up and tie it to the back of the four-wheeler.

There are three more traps to check. They're empty.

Boon and Walter ride past a stretch of once-inhabited land. Dense undergrowth reclaims a cabin on crooked stilts. A chimney and the front facade of another cabin is all that remains. Human debris floats among the marsh reeds. A laundry detergent bottle. A baby's booster seat. A Kentwood water bottle. A paddle to a missing boat. A half-sunk, abandoned car is now only a corroding metal frame. Even the most durable of human impositions is no match for the swamp.

They're almost back to the shed when Boon stops his four-wheeler. Walter pulls up beside him.

"What do we have here," Boon whispers. He points to something up ahead.

Walter knows exactly what he's talking about.

Twenty feet in front of them lays a half-felled slash pine with a rough trunk, tufts of green needles on its branches and thin, short cones.

They both glance at each other. Wide, goofy grins spread out on their faces.

They keep quiet as if out of respect for their sacrificial find. They shake hands instead.

Up close, they see the marks on the bottom of the tree from the stubborn horns or claws of an animal that wanted it down. It's cracked near the bottom of the trunk.

Walter notices the short, straight grains of good pine, ideal for splitting. The surrounding stumps broke its fall. It's close to the ground but not touching. They inspect it for rot and water. It's clean.

They exchange inaudible high fives. Walter pumps his fist in the air.

The thing about pine is that it's a softwood that's considerably hard. It splits easily, but most importantly, it lights easily. It burns with a high, hot flame. Sparks some, not too much smoke. It doesn't burn very long, but it doesn't need to. It's the animal that dies after spawning. It generates enough heat and small throws of flame that it sets the whole thing in motion before its heroic collapse. It's essential to lighting the wood that is going to stay lit.

With Boon's knife they mark where they'll cut with the saw and haul it back to camp. Some pieces need to be big enough to mix with the base. The rest can get smaller from there.

Walter pats Boon on the back, "Wait 'til Collins sees this." He pulls out the canteen and takes a sip. He raises it in a toast, "To my friend, Boon, and his swamp tree."

Boon pats the trunk of the tree like it's the head of a loyal dog that's just dropped the day's hunt, or the cooling carcass itself.

O N SUNDAY NIGHT, WALTER AND Phoebe sit in their downstairs den with moss-colored walls and walnut-stained furniture. A distant, joyful murmur is just under the mahogany planks of the floor, now covered with a thick, thistle rug.

An electric fountain, no bigger than a shoe box, is plugged next to Phoebe's love seat. The water slides down a slate wall, trickles onto smooth rocks. It's then sucked back up to the top to fall again. It's Phoebe's soothing machine.

Walter doesn't like how he can hear the pump gurgle each time the water is recirculated. After a few minutes, he says what he always says, "It's choking on its own supply." But he knows what it means for it to be on. She won't laugh at his jokes.

She's spread out in a ratty pair of pajama pants and an old Tulane sweatshirt with a hole in the armpit. Her lounge wear, an outfit she'd never admit to wearing. Her hair is in a loose ponytail. Her glasses, down on the bridge of her nose.

Her dial is turned so low she's on a frequency all her own.

Walter stretches out in his brown, leather recliner and opens the box of Dunked Doodles, his favorite sugar-coated o's cereal. He eats a handful and reaches for the remote. He turns on the news with volume barely audible.

"Do you want to talk about it?" he says.

"Not really." She flips through one of her many architectural digest magazines. Cabins in the Southern Adirondacks, farmhouses in Georgia, bungalows on the Pacific coast. She likes looking into other people's homes.

The fountain spits and sputters before the fall continues. "It needs more water," Walter says.

"She didn't know who I was." Phoebe looks at the fountain instead of him. "I brought her flowers, put them in the vase by the bookshelf. I went to paint her nails her favorite Mama-Shakin'-Red and it frightened her. She couldn't understand what I was trying to do. Or who I was."

"That's horrible," Walter says. "Did you leave?"

"I was about to. I wanted to. But I sat there and watched some soap with the volume off while this, this Jell-O mold of my mother watched the wall." She goes back to her magazine, snapping each page.

Walter reaches his hand into the cereal box, shovels some into his mouth. "Is the television too loud?"

"No."

The fountain coughs and the motor's wheels whine before the stream is recycled.

"Walter?" Phoebe has a way of making a locked door seem open. Light feeds through her voice.

"Yes."

"The sound of you eating that cereal is disgusting."

The space in which they may connect shifts.

Walter can't keep up. He thinks of how the river is only thirty-five feet deep right outside of Baton Rouge. And by the time it reaches the Moonwalk in the French Quarter, its depth is more than two hundred feet.

He puts the handful of cereal back in the box and brushes the sugar from his pants. He leans back in his chair and listens to the newscaster tell him tomorrow there will be rain.

"Maybe we should get out of town for Christmas," he says. Claudine will be with her in-laws, and Jolie is going skiing with friends. "We could go to that resort in Biloxi."

"I don't want to leave her." Phoebe tosses the magazine into the stack and picks up a new one. "I wished her dead. The whole time I was sitting there."

Walter waits for her to say more. She doesn't. He searches for an anecdote.

The only sound in the room is the trickle of the fountain, a creek running past them. An old man at a urinal.

They sink into a silence deep enough to drown in.

Aᴺʏʙᴏᴅʏ ᴡʜᴏ'ꜱ ᴇᴠᴇʀ ꜱᴇᴇɴ ᴀ Walmart parking lot at Christmas time doubts humans have ever had the capacity for reason.

Walter almost hits a straggling child whose mother is more worried about both pushing and pulling shopping carts. The baskets are packed so full, her line of vision is completely blocked, even of her child. A wife pounds the hood of a car as she fights with her husband in between two parked cars. A young girl cries and points to a plastic reindeer head on the ground. An older man yells in the face of an employee about an expired coupon for blankets with arms and feet and drink holders.

This is all on a Monday morning before nine.

Tut called Walter earlier saying that the Walmart on Tchoupitoulas Street had a stack of wooden pallets by their trash dumpster. Tut was late for work and couldn't stop.

Walter isn't on call for another two hours.

A few years ago, Wilvin's daughter, Pauline, was laid off from a Walmart a week after Thanksgiving. The shift before she left, she stacked all the Christmas shipping pallets outside the back door for Walter to pick up. They were in perfect condition. And there was so much of it, almost two cords worth of wood, that they had enough to decorate their creole cottage replica with weatherboards.

They won that year. It was the year Dad and Collins's supply of wood got wet.

Walter pulls around to the back of the parking lot by the dumpsters. He jumps out, leaving his jacket, phone and wallet in the car. He rolls up his sleeves.

By the trash is a mound, maybe twelve feet, of stacked square pallets.

He digs around. Tut was right, most of it is wet or rotted. He snaps off some of the better pieces from the larger pallets and makes a pile.

A young kid in a blue apron comes out to herd shopping carts. He shields his hand over his eyes to block the sun and watches Walter.

"These are trash?" Walter says.

The kid shrugs and continues his work. He pushes a long wobbly line towards the store. Walter hears the occasional scrape of a car.

In his work slacks, Walter climbs onto some of the crates. He steadies himself then goes up a little higher. A liquid of sorts soaks through to his left calf. He smells sawdust and fertilizer and something sour.

Even if Dad and Collins's wood hadn't got wet that year, their pyre was a standard cone. Nothing special. Walter and Wilvin's could have still won.

One of the pallets breaks. Walter's foot slips in between two boards. His pant hem catches and rips. When he frees himself, the crates begin to fall, collapsing around him. Then he's on the ground.

Dad and Collins still couldn't admit it was an honest win, though. Same with the year their fire had to be extinguished because something toxic was burning off the wood they used. The smoke was green-tinted and foul-smelling. Wilvin and Walter's pyre had been simple but sturdy and clean. It stood a chance.

Walter is right, the pallets higher up are dryer and usable.

They're the disposable kind. Probably made of downfall lumber, a mix of virgin and recycled cottonwood. The wood ignites quickly and burns quickly. It's a perfect middle-weight kindling.

He tosses aside any with paint or a strong odor.

The first missed call must have come right after he got out of the car. By the time he's loaded five crates in his truck, Walter has missed three calls from the hospital.

Mr. Marny is back in the emergency room with complications from his last procedure. Stone fragments remained. An infection developed.

"Who's the attending?" Walter asks the resident.

"Dr. Chang, sir, but I thought you'd want to know."

The resident goes over the chart, delivers the updates.

When Dad died, and Collins finally got to the hospital, Walter lied to him. He told Collins he'd been by Dad's side the whole time. Held his hand as he went out. He didn't tell him that Dad died in an empty room without even a stranger to acknowledge the passing of his final, hard-earned breath.

"We then proceeded," the resident says, "with an ultrasound and found residual stone fragments. There is the presence of infection in the right renal—"

"Repeat that last part."

"We proceeded with an ultrasound and found residual stone frag—"

Horns honk from different directions. Walter has driven through a red light on Louisiana Avenue.

When Dad died, Walter was taking a crap in the handicap bathroom of the west wing of the hospital, basement floor.

Dr. Chang has ordered chemolysis by the time Walter has arrived.

They'll irrigate the kidneys with chemical agents to hasten decomposition of the stone so the body can remove it. It's not entirely uncommon for residual fragments to be found after a PNL. Walter is not necessarily at fault.

He passes the nurses' station that is decorated with a small tree, colored lights. Holly tinsel wraps the length of the desk. Below that hang cutouts of snowmen joined at their stick hands. Gold paper stars, snowflakes, and dreidels drop from the ceiling with string. And taped to the glass are felt stockings with patients' names in glitter.

They're recycled decorations, brought out each year, even the stockings.

"The infection?" Walter asks. He goes into the on-call room to change.

"It's under control." A resident, the one with the moon-shaped face, follows close behind him.

"I have to change," Walter looks down at his torn, stained pants. "Car trouble this morning." He takes off his pants and puts on scrubs. "Update," he says through the door.

"They've begun irrigation—"

"Explain the steps, doctor," Walter says to the resident.

"Perfusion was performed with two coaxial catheters, a nephrostomy catheter, and drainage of the irrigant through ureteral catheter."

Dad wanted his ashes spread out over Lake Pontchartrain. So Walter and Collins planned to go out in Collins's shitty boat. When they got out to the pier that day the boat was completely submerged from un-repaired holes. Collins cut the rope right then and there and let it sink. They dumped Dad's ashes from the dock.

"—the catheter was placed as close to the stone as possible to ensure effective flow around it. Irrigation was tested with saline at lowest possible height above kidney level to achieve a flow rate of 100-120 milliliters per hour."

Some of Dad's ashes blew back on the dock. They brushed them into the water. They cursed at the wake of other boats that pushed everything towards the shore. They watched as the current knocked Dad's remains and algae against the rocks.

"—a solution designed to dissolve the stone was then administered."

"Do you know what is in the solution, doctor?" Walter asks.

"Ten percent hemiacidrin, which contains carbonic acid, citric acid, D-gluconic acid and magnesium at a pH of 3.9. Also, I'm supposed to remind you to put in for the Secret Santa."

"What are we going to monitor?"

"Urinary tract infections, obstructions to flow, intrapelvic pressure, magnesium levels."

"Nice work," Walter says. Before he checks on Mr. Marny, he goes to his office to make a call.

Collins picks up on the second ring, "Yel-low?"

"Did you want some of that pine?"

"Is this some type of wooden-horse thing?"

"No."

"Then what is it?"

"We probably won't use it all."

"Thanks, but no. Save it for next—"

"—I won't—"

"—You interested in grabbing dinner this week?" Collins asks.

"What? Ah, this week is no good."

"Then soon."

"Soon." Walter hangs up.

When Walter gets back to the ER, Mr. Marny is coding.

His magnesium levels are elevated. There is obvious swelling of his face and limbs with marked jugular venous distention. His eyes are wide but not discerning when they catch Walter's.

The interns rattle off numbers and degrees, drug names and doses. Walter finds that he can barely move. The language in which they speak has gone foreign. The sounds of the machines, hostile.

"Dr. Doucet?"

"The infection has spread," he manages to say.

"Yes, sir, it appears so. We are going to—"

Walter hears shots fired too far away to be in the hospital. He smells the salty brine and bleach of a gallon barrel holding the head of an alligator. How one polishes a Civil War musket, how one cleans a kill to mount, how one gets wet wood to work to his advantage. Can he not remember these things or were they never his?

"Dr. Doucet?"

They have briefly stabilized Mr. Marny before he goes into cardiac arrest.

He is pronounced dead at 11:49 a.m. on Monday the twelfth of December.

His chart lists no living kin to notify.

In Walter's office, someone has left on his desk a bear holding green and red chocolate balls. It says Happy Ho-Ho-Holidays. Walter opens it up and eats a handful, then puts the bear in the trash.

He sits at his desk and pulls Dad's chart from the bottom drawer. Cardiac complications are listed as the cause of death. He was pronounced at 10:32 a.m. on the twenty-fourth of January. No autopsy was ordered. At the time, Walter didn't want to know.

Now, he wishes one had been done.

In the chart is a signed certificate of cremation.

The funeral pyre. The cosmic death. The careless devour of nature. The body, no different than dried moss or dryer lint. One cheap life makes room for another, Walter thinks.

The entire universe bets against us.

WALTER DRAGS THE CHARCOAL GRILL out into the grass away from his porch and removes the metal grate. From the shed, he grabs a few logs and douses them with lighter fluid. He rolls up a sheet of newspaper and lights it, then holds it to the wood. A blue flame zips along before taking grip.

He remembers Grandpaw telling him about the Aztecs and their New Fire ceremony to stave off the end of the world as one cycle shifted to another. In preparation, the people stopped working, fasted, performed ritual cleansing and bloodletting, destroyed household items, and observed silence.

Walter must have grabbed cedar from the shed, because it smells good and hearty. It wraps around him until he's inside of a cigar humidor. The kind he didn't know about until he was a grown man. Dad stashed his cheap cigars in the freezer.

The Aztecs sacrificed a man at sunset on the last day of the year, on an extinct volcano, and a fire was placed on his chest. It was the only fire allowed to be lit. When the first sparks sprang from the dead man's chest, a new calendar began and a huge bonfire was lit.

Walter's fire eats the corners of the paper first, then works from the inside out. He takes a pair of meat tongs, moves the wood around, and adds a little more.

He made the call this morning. He's taken a leave of absence, a period to regain confidence. He'll return to work after the New Year. His supervisor thought it was a good idea.   "Anything I should be worried about?" Phoebe asked at breakfast.

"Not a thing," Walter said, despite his face saying otherwise. She kissed him on the forehead then left for work.

Walter then called the only person he knows who doesn't work until four on Wednesdays. "Boon, what do you think about Christmas colors?"

"I like it," he said.

Boon stands in walter's backyard, drinking a Dixie beer. "Should be here by Friday, Monday at the latest," he says. Boon's sister called that morning about some diseased honey locusts that had been brought down and quarantined.

"She says she sent down the better part of two, three trees."

Walter adds another small log to the grill. An old CCR tape plays on the boom box.

"I'm going to go pick it up from a guy out near LaPlace."

"You need help?" Walter says.

"We might need a few of us. Not sure how big they're going to be."

The honey locust is a hardwood, a heavyweight. It has thorny branches and a burst of yellow leaves in the fall. It'd make strong support beams for their pyre, depending on how big the pieces are. They'll mix the rest throughout, strategically placing it on top of the softwoods, so it is able to slowly heat before igniting. Honey locust is fairly easy to chop and light.

Its heating value is what's impressive, 25.8 million Btu per cord.

"We can't do better than that right now," Walter says. "It's exactly what we needed." He holds his can up for Boon to tap. He takes a sip of his beer, wipes his mouth with the neck of his flannel shirt. He needs to shower and shave.

Walter goes into the shed and brings out two coffee canisters he's prepared. He holds them up, "Christmas X and Christmas Y."

He opens the first canister. Sawdust soaked in strontium chloride then dried. It's a common salt compound. Walter got it from the pet store, where it was advertised to clean fish aquariums.

Walter takes a handful of the sawdust and tosses it into the fire.

The flame lashes out a crimson red then licks it back.

"How'd you do that?" Boon says.

He takes another handful and only sprinkles it on the fire this time. A red flame crawls halfway up the pit and then back down.

Walter hands the second canister to Boon. It's sawdust soaked in copper sulfate, which is also a salt compound. The hardware store sells it as an algaecide for garden ponds or backyard pools.

Boon takes a handful and throws it into the fire. A blaze of green flashes.

"It's a freakin' Christmas miracle," Boon says.

They both take a handful of sawdust from their canisters and throw it in at the same time. A nasty brown flame creeps up then falls away.

They then take turns. Red. Green. Red. Green. Christmas.

They decide to soak some of the smaller logs in the colored solutions then stagger them in the crown. They'll also use pine cones and do the same. They'll be able to stuff the pine cones along the outside of the pyre to quickly glow then fade.

"I've got an idea," Boon says.

"Shoot."

"Never mind." Boon finishes his beer and crumples the can.

"What is it?"

Boon leans in a little. "My neighbor used to make Christmas gifts for everyone out of pine cones, decorate them, and she used to spray cinnamon oil on them. They'd smell so good. I smell that and it's Christmas."

"Then we scent the pine cones," Walter says.

Both men stand watching as the fire attempts its impossible climb.

Walter thinks of the Bonfire of the Vanities. During the Mardi Gras Festival of 1497, in an effort to purge their souls, the people of Florence, Italy, collected things such as books, art, mirrors, cosmetics, hairbrushes, and fancy clothes, and publicly burned them.

Fire was their mediator for redemption. It was their agent of purity, incapable of polluting itself.

Boon gathers a few pine cones from the yard and tosses one in the fire. The resin quickly catches into a vibrating blaze.

"Jesus, Boss," Boon says. He stands next to Walter, poking the pine cones with the meat tongs. "Maybe we need to get you some cinnamon oil. Or go ahead and put your shirt in the fire. I'm not even standing that close to you."

"Watch it, kid."

"I could get the hose. Spray you down?"

Walter wrestles his arms around him.

"Mercy," Boon says, pretending to gasp for air. "Mercy."

Walter hears a truck pull into the driveway. He and Boon walk to the front of the house and find Collins climbing out of it.

"Whose truck?" Walter says.

"Borrowed it from a friend." Collins gets out in a T-shirt and jeans. "Did you hear?"

"Hear what?"

"Someone had another go at the house last night. Probably teenagers. They broke more than they took."

Walter hadn't heard anything.

"I went ahead and got some stuff out." Collins pulls back a tarp from the bed of the truck. It's mostly furniture. The Victrola. The dining room chairs. The chest of drawers. "Even brought you that," Collins says, pointing to the kitchen table. "You know."

"What are you going to do with it?" Walter asks.

"Pick what you want. I'm going to put the rest in my garage for now, I guess." Collins puts on a pair of very white workman's gloves and walks to the back of the truck. He opens the back, begins to unhook the straps holding everything down.

"You going to try and burn it?" Walter says.

"What do you take me for?"

Collins stands in the back of the truck like he's the first to the top of a hill. "Where the hell are your Christmas decorations?"

Walter took down the lights and hasn't put up new ones yet.

"I'll take the chest of drawers."

"Really? What for? Need a place to store your dinosaur pajamas and Dungarees? I was going to give it to Remy." Collins uses his grandson as a trump card any chance he gets.

"Fine. Fine. Then the table."

Before Boon leaves for work, he gives Walter and Collins a hand hoisting it down. They haul it to the garage and set it down in a corner.

"Want a beer?" Walter says.

"Anything," Collins says. He takes off the gloves and shoves them in his back pocket. Then he walks around the garage as if taking inventory.

"Nothing is yours," Walter says.

"I used to have a saw with that exact handle."

"Not yours."

Walter can't remember the last time Collins had a beer at his place. He hands him a Dixie.

"What were you two doing back here?" Collins asks, circling the grill.

The fire now, is just a low, unimpressive red glow.

"Just heatin' up the old mittens," Walter says and claps his gloved hands together.

"Liar." Collins picks up the meat tongs and moves around what's left of the logs.

"How's the building coming along?" Walter says.

Collins picks up a handful of dried leaves. "When did it get so hard to find good wood?" He breaks off pieces and puts them in the grill. The fire doesn't grow. The leaves singe and shrivel into ash.

They watch as the fire becomes nothing but a thin stream of smoke.

"Remember when Wilvin and I built the USS Louisiana?"

"Damn straight I do. God, that thing was a beauty. Who helped y'all with that?"

"That guy from Wilvin's work. The one fired for touching the women. Wasn't much with the ladies, but he could just about make anything out of a piece of wood and a carving knife."

Collins coughs on his beer and lets out a thick laugh, the kind a younger brother can't help but want. "What the hell was that guy's name?"

"Copshaw or something."

Collins finishes his beer and tosses it into the grill. It just sits there. The fire is out.

"Wasn't much of a bonfire," Walter says.

"You could've gotten if off the ground. You gave up too soon." Collins plucks the can out of the grill with his index finger. He walks over to the trash and lifts the lid. He pretends to shoot and score.

"Wood was overcrowded," Walter says.

"It was too much of a beauty to burn," Collins says.

"True."

Walter can feel Collins staring at him.

"You good?" Collins says.

Walter is able to avoid eye contact for about a minute. Then he's caught.

"You good?"

"Yeah, I'm good," Walter says.

Collins wraps his arm around Walter, squeezes his neck.

"Stop."

"You sure you don't want anything else?" Collins says about the furniture in the truck.

"I'm sure."

Walter watches Collins secure the straps in the back of the truck. Then Collins peels away from the curb like a teenager from a bad party.

Walter goes into the shed and kneels down in front of the table. He runs his hand over the smooth wood. He realizes that it probably can be salvaged. He can replace two of the legs, put on a fourth. It won't matter if the wood doesn't match. He can cut out the rotted part in the middle and repair it with a fresh piece of cedar or maybe even some of the oak.

Walter thinks of the year the USS Louisiana wouldn't light, '88. Collins and Dad had built a Santa standing on something that looked like a soapbox. Santa's bag of toys, slung over his shoulder, became a large ball of fire within twenty minutes. It broke away and rolled down the levee, heading towards the table with food. People screamed and ran. A few of the women, Beccalyn included, grabbed their trays of cookies or bowls of eggnog, before escaping.

Santa's fireball swerved and missed the table, smacked two cars, then sat smoking in the middle of the road. People ran over with brooms and large sticks. Someone grabbed a tarp.

It died out like a vicious animal who's attacked an entire clan and is then brought down.

"Thank God no one got hurt," they said to each other, eyes wide with shock.

"You okay?" the more shaken ones said.

That's when one sound finally cleared through the commotion. It had been there the entire time.

Dad clapping. He stood in his bomber hat next to the charred Santa, only the soapbox burning at its feet, encouraging a finale.

Early thursday evening, Walter finds Phoebe at the kitchen table. She has lit the candles of the hand-made, German pyramid. The smoke from the candles spin the fan, which sends the red, wooden dolls revolving around a Christmas tree. On the radio, a choir sings, No more let sins and sorrows grow. Nor thorns infest the ground.

"What are we sending this year?" Walter says.

Phoebe holds up one of their Christmas cards. A sleigh drawn through the snow on a winter's night.

"Doesn't the horse look a little tired?"

Phoebe opens the card, Season's Greetings.

"I'm not sure that's expressed," Walter says.

Her laughter is the slow building of light in winter. He remembers the feeling of savoring the wait. Moonbeams unfold from her parted lips. "It's December. Somber is warmth," she says. Even she can't keep a straight face.

She carefully loops the ends of each surname and street name. She licks an envelope and presses it securely down. Then she stacks it with the rest.

"Can I help?" Walter says and sits down next to her. He picks up a pen.

Phoebe takes the pen and hands him the roll of stamps.

He hates the taste of stamps, but he licks and sticks anyway.

Walter holds up one of the envelopes. "The Dancys still live in that townhouse in Algiers?"

"I know. They love temporary living."

"It's been seventeen years. Wait, wasn't he diagnosed last year?"

"Remission."

They both try hard not to laugh. "No, it's wrong," Phoebe says, teeth clenched.

"So wrong."

"He's been talking about dying since we were in our late twenties."

Their bodies shake with laughter before it finally spills out.

Phoebe waves her hand in front of her tearing eyes.

"And this guy," she says holding up an envelope. "Never has there been a sadder sack."

"Oh, poor Ralph." He's the husband of Phoebe's college roommate, Bitsy. He shuffles around with slouched shoulders and hair sagging in one limp chunk of hairspray. "How many uniforms does he own?" Walter asks about the only outfit he's seen him wear: white, wrinkled shirt and grey, cuffed slacks.

"What do you call him?"

"My one-martini man. After that, sweat gathers on his upper lip and temples, his mouth flaps faster than a broken bike chain."

Phoebe releases a full-throated, head back, hyena-laugh. A blaze of light rips through Walter.

When Collins first met Phoebe at the bonfire of '78, he said she had a nice laugh. Walter knows that's not the first thing he noticed. He watched Collins look at her. Phoebe has always been a sight.

"New Iberia?" Walter says. "When did they move there?"

"They started building it when Lane was a senior." Their son is a year younger than Claudine.

A caustic rendition of the Twelve Yats of Christmas comes on the radio.

"Let's do it," Walter slaps down an envelope. "If we leave now we can make the caroling in Jackson Square." He picks up the phone and dials Claudine's number. "Hell, we can sing better than this," he points to the radio. "A Crawfish dey Caught in Arabi." Phoebe tries to join in but is laughing too hard. The phone rings on the other line.

Claudine's answering machine picks up.

"—Should I leave a message?" Walter says. "What should I say?"

"Say…say—"

Walter hangs up.

"Why'd you do that?" Phoebe says.

"I couldn't think of what to say. They aren't home."

"You should have…"

"We wouldn't have enough time to get down there and park."

Phoebe picks up the pen and begins to write another address. She stops, tears up the envelope. She lets the pieces fall to the floor. She starts again. "Dammit," she says and tears up another.

Phoebe sits at the table and stares at the stack of envelopes. "I haven't talked to some of these people in years. If I ran into some of them tomorrow, I'm not sure I'd even recognize them." She pushes her chair away from the table and stands up.

"Where are you going?" Walter asks.

"I promised Jolie I'd bring her by a bag of her warmer clothes."

"Do you want me to ride with you?"

"I'm just dropping them off with her roommate."

"OK," Walter says, not wanting to impose. On what? He's not sure.

Phoebe kisses him on the top of the head, no different than she does Pierre, and leaves.

Walter decides to go to Audubon Park to look for downed branches. He parks on St. Charles and walks along the side of the park, near Exposition Boulevard. He follows a dirt-marked runner's trail. Occasionally, he has to step, or jump, out of the way when someone says, Coming up on your left, and speeds past him.

He begins to gather the fallen branches of a live oak. Sometimes when burned, oak smells of licorice.

He stops under another large oak. The branches span longer than the height of the tree. Gnarly, flailing branches fight against gravity. They are heavy and tired, doing a final voodoo wave, some gris gris, wordless chant. The limbs dip down like the loop of Henle then curl back to the sky.

An entire copse of two-hundred-year-old oaks can exist because a squirrel planted a single acorn. The trees share a complex, tangled root system.

The oak is draped in Spanish moss, sprouted with resurrection ferns. It is a sturdy tree. Tolerant to flood and drought. Defiant against wind, resistant to fire. The oak is reverence preserved in the mute of time.

Walter gathers the smaller stuff. Middleweight, kindling size. Oak's heating efficiency is 24 to 28 Btu with a density of 37 to 58 pounds per cubic feet.

"—Coming up on your right," a runner says. Walter accidently moves to the right. He bumps the runner with an armful of sticks.

"Watch it," the guy says.

"Sorry. Sorry." Walter picks up what he's dropped.

The last dying light of the day filters through the thick canopy of the park's trees. It gets dark quick. There are some people out. A dog runs up to an oak and lifts its hind leg. Then runs barking back to its owner who clips its leash. Two woman joggers run past him talking about mutual funds and fixed fees. A dad and two sons carry home their whiffle balls and bats. One of the boys wears his glove on his head.

Walter walks to where Hurst Street hits the park. His hands are full. He decides to head back to the car when he thinks he sees Phoebe's car. Would she park this far from the dorms?

He walks towards it, unable to tell if she's sitting in it. He gets closer and sees it's empty. It's definitely hers. The Tulane bumper sticker. The plastic Mardi Gras cup with lipsticked-straw in the holder. Her files of listings in the back seat. A yard sign and mallet on the floorboard.

He thinks of leaving a note tucked in the wiper. He has no paper. He walks up the street a ways in hopes of finding her For Sale sign and surprising her.

He walks up three or four blocks and back. There are no signs.

Feeling the full weight of the oak in his arms, Walter walks back to his car.

The holy fire occurs annually in Jerusalem. The Greek Orthodox chant, "Kyrie eleison, Kyrie eleison," Lord, have mercy, as the priest enters the Tomb of Jesus without any means to make fire.

Spontaneously, thirty-three white candles light.

It's believed to be the resurrection flame. A miracle.

And it is. Just not the sacred tongues, religious type. It's one of nature's grand illusions. Her death-before-life trick. A fern grows up through a decaying building. Algae forms on a sunken boat. And from the cold darkness, a warm flame.

Walter pictures himself standing in front of his pyre. His arms outstretched, presenting his miracle. The tower behind him taking everything from the night as it erupts into fire all on its own.

The fire-worshipper knows phosphorus. So do members of the military, pyromaniacs, and meth heads. It must first be dissolved in an organic solvent, which will take time to evaporate, delaying the inevitable.

Phosphorus self-ignites when coming into contact with oxygen.

Walter imagines commanding his bonfire with just his presence. He is Vulcan, Agni, Gerra, Hephaestus.

He is standing with an armful of sticks in a darkening park, wishing for a heavily controlled substance to impress his wife of thirty years.

Twenty-six million americans suffer from kidney disease. That number continues to grow alongside the obesity epidemic that affects one third of all adults.

Things appear to be getting worse.

Walter pulls up to the window to retrieve his bag of tacos and a medium drink. By eight o'clock on Saturday night, Phoebe still wasn't home from work. Walter couldn't get in touch with her, so he decided to eat dinner alone.

He eats the tacos in his parked car next to Audubon Park. He's hoping to find some downed branches, good-sized ones that he can season. Instead of entering the park the same way he did the other night, he decides to drive down Calhoun Street and enter from one of the side streets that ends at the park. He wants to cover new ground.

That's not entirely true. He wants to see if Phoebe's car is, for the third night in a row, parked on Hurst Street.

It's not.

It's parked on Calhoun Street, not far from where it was before. It's in front of a house with four alligators pulling an inflatable Santa in a pirogue across the lawn.

The house is completely dark. There is not a For Sale sign in the yard, or on the houses next door. There are no lock boxes.

Walter drives all the way down Calhoun until he reaches Camp Street. He doesn't pass a single realty sign.

Contradictions accumulate. The amygdala activates.

Walter circles around the block and parks his car in view of hers. His organs can't seem to figure out their function. His bladder is racing, his mind needs release.

There's an unexpected socioeconomic correlation with renal stones. The higher the economic standing, the higher the risk.

Walter keeps the engine running.

Another odd fact finds his ear. It's doing the thinking now. The increased incidents of kidney stones in the Southeast, earned the region the name "stone belt."

Walter shakes the ice in his cup, drains the last of the soda through the straw.

His spleen takes over, surprised that asparagus, cauliflower, spinach or mushrooms do not lower the urinary pH or decrease uric acid excretion, which invites stone growth.

Walter gets out of the car. He leaves the door open, the lights on, the bell dinging. He goes up to Phoebe's car and peeks in. To make sure it's hers. It is. It's hers.

He finds himself sneaking back to his car, half-running, half-tiptoeing. He jumps in and slams the door. Pulls out of there fast.

Both hands grip the wheel as he takes the first left he can, away from Calhoun. What's the homeostasis goal? He asks himself over and over. The homeostasis goal?

He should know this. There should be no second guessing. Go. Home—

Restore intravascular volume and blood pressure to maintain perfusion of essential organs.

He takes a left on their street. His lungs are the first to get it right. They take a deep breath.

An unusual number of streetlights are burnt out on Coliseum. The neighbors' driveways have a menacing glow.

His phone buzzes on the passenger seat. He scrambles for it, readying himself to sound nonchalant when she says hello.

"I know how to do it," a voice slurs.

"Collins?"

"If a coyote attacks. I remembered. I know how to survive."

"Where are you?"

"Do you know what to do?"

"I pull the trigger of my gun. Where are you?"

Collins lists three places, the casino, a crab shack out by the lake, and someplace downtown Walter has never heard of, before telling him where he really is. A bar on Tulane Avenue.

"Stay put," Walter says and pulls back out of his driveway.

He thinks of the first time he had a drink. Out on the back porch of the Vacherie house. He couldn't have been more than twelve, thirteen. Collins had stolen it from the stash near the TV. It was a brown liquor in a label-less bottle. It was liquid fire. Scorched Walter from his tongue to his intestines. He thought he could still feel it when it hit his bladder, burn when he pissed it out. That was just from a few swigs.

Collins could take it without flinching. Drank probably an eighth of the bottle before he was hanging over the back steps in between the screen door and the frame, puking every last shred of anything he had in him.

Walter walks in the bar to find Collins talking it up with a square-jawed man, his hat pulled low, about the upkeep of greens on a course, the ideal peripheral landscape. At first glance Collins appears to be sober and the man, listening.

"Walt, you remember when that golf course, when wild animals just walked onto the course. Tell him, tell Garry here, about the time I saw a—"

"—Let me give you a ride home."

"You kidding me?" Collins starts to talk louder, stands up from the stool. "I didn't call my kid brother for a ride." He jabs Walter hard on the shoulder. "I just wanted to have a drink with him. Needed someone to collob…corrobor…collaborate my stories.

"A shot of whiskey for my brother," Collins tells the bartender.

"Does Beccalyn know you're here?"

"Yeah, she sent me." Collins laughs at himself.

"Let's go."

"What does it take to get you to have a drink with me?" Collins turns to the rest of the bar, "My own brother."

A few of the patrons glance at them, but it's a place where nobody looks that far past their own drink.

The bartender sets the shot down. Walter doesn't drink it.

"Go on. Get out of here if you're going to be like that," Collins says.

Someone's put on an Elvis song, probably the woman who now grinds her backside against a disinterested man. She dances with her eyes closed while the man watches a young girl shoot pool. A few stools down, an old man in a half-buttoned shirt tries to sell the bartender lawn furniture. "Durable stuff," he keeps saying. "It'll last."

Walter gets up and drops money on the bar for the shot that Collins drinks.

"Nice to meet you," he says to Collins's new friend, who is too busy picking slimy nuts out of a wooden dish to notice.

He pats Collins on the shoulder and leaves.

Walter waits in the parking lot for almost an hour. He tries to find something other than Christmas music that isn't static. The soft rock station works until the break.

-Lucky caller, what do you wish for?

-The room my wife and I spent our honeymoon sixteen years ago, overlooking Blue Canyon Ranch.

-I think we can make something happen.

-It burned down in a fire five years ago, lost all their horses.

-We've got something better in store for you.

-Really? Oh really? Really? What?

-Who's your favorite station this holiday season?

The man was the tenth caller, won two free tickets to an all-inclusive Caribbean cruise for him and his motion-sickness-prone wife. Walter has never heard a winner ask if there is something else he could have instead. Something with horses. The man's wife likes looking at horses. The call goes off air after that. "Deck the Halls" comes on and Walter changes the station.

The bar door opens and Collins comes stumbling out.

Walter flickers the car's headlights. Halfway to the car, Collins kneels down on the gravel and vomits. The muscles of his back ripple with each heave. He wipes his mouth with the collar of his shirt and struggles to his feet.

He climbs into the passenger seat, smelling of whiskey, peppers, and bile. "Drive slow," he says.

The Pontchartrain Expressway unfurls against the New Orleans skyline. They spit past the Superdome, the barbed-wire gates of the prison, the cemeteries.

Hank Williams sings about being lonesome.

"You gonna tell me what's going on?" Walter says.

Collins leans back his head and closes his eyes.

They pull up in front of Collins's house. It's beige with large columns and a flat roof. Neoclassical and similar to all the other homes in the Lakeview cul-de-sac. Collins and Beccalyn designed the interior layout when it was built ten years ago. A television over the tub, a walk-in closet that joins the bedroom to the bath, a special laundry chute that sends dirty socks straight to the basement.

"Wanna come in for a beer?" Collins asks.

"Too late," Walter says, even though it's before eleven.

"Pussy."

The front yard has a giant inflatable snow globe. Some fan inside keeps the fake snow blowing around, falling on plastic homes and trees. A stuffed Santa is coming out of a water meter hole that Beccalyn has made of foam. Mrs. Claus sits on the porch with her feet up and a cat in her lap.

"Just read an article about coyotes snatching pets in St. Tammany." Collins fumbles with the seatbelt. Walter helps him. "Got this man's dog right out from under him." He stumbles out of the car. He shuts the door three times before the light finally goes off.

He waves and then motions for Walter to roll down the window.

"What?"

"How'd you survive?" Collins has a big fake smirk on his face. His eyes are heavy.

"Aren't they more scared of us?"

Collins starts up the walkway like he's going to make Walter pry it out of him. He turns around halfway and in a whisper that isn't a whisper says, "They have weak ribs. Go after the ribs."

"Good to know."

Collins gets to the porch and sits down in one of the rocking chairs. The automatic sensor turns on the porch light. Collins pulls a cigar from his shirt pocket. He bites off the end and spits it into a potted plant. He tries to light it but his lighter is empty.

"Go inside," Walter says.

Collins waves him on and searches his pockets for another light.

Walter taps the horn, holds up both a lighter and matches from his cup holder, and drives off with Collins giving him the finger.

Walter wakes on sunday morning to rain on the windows forming oblique patterns on the bedsheets, the walls. It's still early.

Not wanting to move, he stares at their dresser. Its marble top hosts a perpetual reunion between his and hers. Her Spanish fan spreads out in front of his old bottle of cologne. His lost cuff links find shelter in a jar next to the broken bulbs of her earrings, safety pins and thread. Her retired Mardi Gras mask watches over the patina dish with his pocket change and past receipts. Her grandmother's debut crown rides on top of his tin streetcar that hides his grandfather's flask.

Shadows of rain run along the floorboards and over the mismatched tiles of the fireplace.

When Phoebe's hand slowly comes over him, strokes his forearm, he stiffens. She holds him from behind.

What does it take, Walter thinks, for light and heat to be liberated from a piece of wood? Before combustion can happen, a substance has to reach its ignition point, its kindling temperature. For the burning to begin? Depends. How much oxygen is in the air?

When she starts up the side of his ear, he submits.

He rolls over to find her eyes barely cracked open, a half-smile that quickly falls.

He tries to kiss her neck where she likes it, along the common carotid artery. She won't lift her chin high enough for him to get there.

Their touching is tangential. They must go through former selves to get to each other.

They don't take off their clothes. Just move them aside.

Walter climbs on top, nudging and then thrusting. Sleep sweat mixes with new sweat, his and hers. It smears together on small patches of exposed skin. Wrist to bicep. Lower thigh to inner thigh.

They make a sweet and sour smell like the drowned, dying roots of a ginger plant after a large storm.

She gazes at him. When their eyes meet, hers wander to the gathered material of the tester canopy.

He focuses on the bedpost.

Walter pumps mechanically, like a manual miter saw. One that he is operating with someone else's arm, upper torso.

They swim in humidity.

The air outside the comforter is contracted with winter cold. It catches a socked foot, nips at an ankle. Walter pulls the blanket back over them.

It slides back to the side. Cold air on their legs. Walter repositions the blanket.

He can feel himself a mile ahead of her, riding out on a crest. Leaving her to bob in open water.

"Wait," she says.

There is nothing he can do about it.

His orgasm putters out like a dying car in the middle of a nowhere road.

Walter lies next to her, trying to catch his breath.

He offers to help her finish. But she has stopped swimming, refuses to paddle.

There is a crack outside of the window. Water gushes from the side of the roof and down the window.

It casts a wash down the wall and onto a bronze flambeau carrier in the corner, who in mid-dance lights the way.

"We need a new gutter," Phoebe says.

"It just needs to be cleaned out," Walter says. "Emptied."

They regress into remote regions of themselves.

On Sunday afternoon Phoebe has an open house. Walter has an LSU versus Alabama game.

"Whatcha got for me, Boss?" Boon says. He's come through the back door without knocking. Walter gets him a beer.

"There's a big house over on Danneel Street that's being renovated, thought we might check it out."

"Sounds good." Boon picks up a framed picture on the end table. "These your girls?"

It's an Easter picture from a few years back, outside of St. George's Church with Phoebe's mother. Phoebe had bribed them to go with the promise of a big brunch afterwards. "That's them."

"Lucky for them, they didn't get your looks," Boon says.

"Watch it, son." Walter hands Boon a bowl of chips.

"They ever help with the bonfire?"

"They weren't ever really interested. My dad would have thought it sacrilegious anyway. It was what the men did," Walter says in a mocking tone. There was one year when he thought Jolie might be hooked. She had just turned fourteen and talked about the fire for a month straight. Turned out it was a friend of her cousin, who was helping to build, that she was interested in.

Boon joins Walter on the leather couch. The score is three to zero, Alabama. Walter thinks of the almost perfect game Collins pitched his sophomore year at LSU against Grambling. His concentration broke somewhere in the top half of the eighth inning and a batter drove it out to left field. They scored five runs that inning.

"What the hell happened out there?" Dad said afterwards.

"Arm got tired." Collins said. Walter knew. He saw Beccalyn and a girlfriend sit in the bleachers sometime during the seventh inning. Who couldn't hear that woman's machine-gun laugh? They started dating soon after that.

During a commercial, Walter asks, "How's Alma?"

"Difficult."

This is the extent of their conversation until 'Bama beats LSU, 21-17.

They decide to take Walter's truck because the bed is bigger. As they walk down the driveway, Walter points to the sagging gutter with bits of pine cones, needles, leaves. "I got to figure out how to get up there. Clean those out."

Boon stops and looks up at the gutter, "Looks like you got a bit of a squirrel problem."

"No, just clogged."

"Who do you think is piling that stuff up? That's a nest."

"Crap," Walter says.

"Don't you have someone you can call, Doctor?"

"Smartass."

They get in the car and drive towards the house Walter found when he was out the other night looking. If Phoebe is not home, he goes out driving, looking for wood. He occasionally circles back by the house. If she's home, he goes in. If not, he drives more. He doesn't have to ask where she's been if he walks in last.

"You heard from your sister?"

"Not yet."

"Think we'll get them?"

"Sure. Quarantined trees can be serious. Might just take a little longer."

"We still got time left."

"You worried, Boss?"

"Still plenty of time."

"'Cause I can call her, see if there's a tracking number for it—"

"—You're all about it today, huh?" Walter lightly thrusts his fist into Boon's thick arm.

The Hank Williams station from the night before has turned into some Appalachian folk music. A man with a register too high sings about bears and sailing on a moonless night. The song sounds as disjointed as its subject matter.

"Are we really listening to this?" Boon says.

"Oh right, I've heard what you listen to, Grandpa. Don't judge me."

"Hey old man, can we listen to somethin' with a beat?"

Boon changes the station to a man rapping about his blue jeans, a futon, and female parts. Walter pretends he knows the song, mouths it to the minivan that pulls up along the passenger side.

The woman frowns. Boon shakes his head like he's never met Walter before. The woman drives off.

"A buddy of mine," Boon says, "had this skinny little squirrel in his backyard that kept moving this one, darn acorn back and forth between these two trees. Back and forth. Back and forth. Same two holes in the same two trees. Just as soon as it dropped the nut in one hole, it picked it right back up and brought it to the other one. It did this for like three days straight. Anytime my buddy looked outside, it was doing it. Wouldn't stop. Squirrels lock in when they find a good place. You wanna get rid of them, put some cayenne on a few Brazil nuts and make 'em easy to find."

"Brazil nuts?"

"Trust me."

The gate to a gutted Victorian house is open. They walk up the driveway, giving a few cautionary hellos. No need to spook a man with a power tool. All they find is one man listening to a cassette headset while carving detail into a staircase banister.

"That's some good-looking design," Boon says. He puts his hand out for the man to shake.

They explain what they're looking for. Any wood that's going to be tossed.

"All I can speak for is the old staircase," the man says, "But you don't want it. Even if you're just burning it. Trust me." He motions over to the dumpster. A blue tarp is tied down over it.

They walk over to the dumpster giving each other the not it look.

Walter barely lifts the edge of the tarp and peeks in first. There is a staircase-looking mound of wood with holes, shredded bases, parts of it probably hollow.

Thick piles of clear insect wings cover the wood.

Walter shudders and closes the tarp. "Are they on me?" He brushes his hair, feeling like brown bugs will fall from it. "Are they on me?" He dances away from the dumpster, shaking out his clothes.

"What is it?" Boon says and takes a look. "Termites."

Walter's phone buzzes. It's a text from Phoebe. She's working late.

He ignores it, kicks the dumpster instead. "Termites." He kicks it again. "Shit." And again.

"Boss? Boss? Relax. There's not even that much wood there."

The carver has taken off his headphones and is standing with his arms crossed.

"We're leaving," Boon says.

"Probably should," the carver says.

Walter is still cursing to himself when they get in the car.

"You okay?" Boon says.

"Yeah. Fine."

"We weren't going to get much from it anyway."

"We need a big find. We need support beams. We need more—"

"—We'll find it."

They drive trailing a silence like bad dust.

Walter pulls up to his house to let Boon out. "I'm going to go get squirrel supplies," he says.

"I'm telling you: cayenne, Brazil nuts, done."

"And it worked for your buddy?"

"What? Who?"

"The acorn mover?"

"Nah, no way. He finally just shot that squirrel. Put it out of its misery." Boon taps the side of the car as Walter pulls away.

He does go to Winn-Dixie and get cayenne and nuts and almost fights with a woman who leaves her basket at the register to find one more item. Then he takes the long way home and drives down Calhoun Street.

Something has burrowed itself in Walter, is beginning to eat from the inside, out.

Walter inches down Calhoun until he finds her car. This time it's farther towards Prytania Street. It's in front of a white house with simple green garlands wrapped around the banisters, red ribbons tied on the doors.

The sun is setting and the house looks washed in a light purple.

He drives slowly by her car, peering into the passenger side. On the seat are fliers, a potted plant, and a half-eaten tray of cookies from the open house.

She's carelessly left one of the windows cracked. What if it rains? Walter thinks. Then what? Then what? He finds himself glancing around, worried she'll catch him.

This time he pulls the car a little ways in front of hers. He adjusts the rearview mirror to watch her car. He still can't turn off the engine.

The warm air blows on Walter until he is made of the night.

He wakes to dry mouth and the sound of rain splattering against the window. Phoebe's car is missing from the review mirror. He checks the side mirrors.

She's gone.

Walter's car is dead.

He'll have to call someone.

Eggs. Larvae. Nymph. Winged. It really is as they say, guilt is a termite son-of-a—

EVEN IN WINTER, NEW ORLEANS finds its heavy Caribbean night, its thick throat-clear of an evening.

Walter stands in his backyard. The floodlights have come on even though it's not fully dark yet.

From the shed, Walter has pulled the oak from the park, Wilvin's cypress, the pine, some of the sweetgum branches, and some small piles of wood that his crew has dropped off: beech, more pine, some maple and sycamore. All good wood just a little too wet.

A simple method to determine if firewood is dry. Strike two pieces together. A dull thud means too much moisture. A sharp crack, the wood is fairly dry.

Moisture collects along wood grains. The longer the grains, the more moisture the wood retains. Walter has cut the pieces into ideal length, 1.5 feet. The base pieces, he's left longer.

He glides a knife along the log, peeling strips of bark off. Whittling the skin of the wood allows it to purge its moisture faster. For the branches that were too thin, some of the oak and the sweetgum, he just cuts long slits in them, hopes it does the trick.

At five p.m. on Monday, as planned, Collins walks up the driveway. He stands watching without saying anything.

Walter takes the ax and brings it down hard on some of the thicker, wetter pieces. He splits them in two.

"You're going to need to help me haul it," Collins finally says.

"I figured." Walter brings the ax down harder.

That was the deal. Collins came and jumped his car, and Walter seasons Collins's half of the cypress Wilvin let them split.

Walter follows behind him out to the truck, watching the thinning patch of hair on the back of his head. Wilvin already cut most of the wood.

"How's work?" Walter says.

"Good."

They haul the wood to the backyard.

In a patch of dirt, Walter builds a small fire with leaves, paper, bark and kindling. He rolls rocks from their fish-less pond to circle the fire and leans the wood against them.

The small fire smokes three times it size.

"Where's Phoebe?"

"With her mother."

Every five minutes they rotate the wood to season thoroughly. It takes about a half hour for it to dry out enough to burn.

Collins digs his hands in his pockets. "You going to tell me what last night was about?"

Walter feeds the fire. "Car died."

"What were you doing?"

"I was parked there. Left on my lights by accident when I went searching in Audubon."

Walter rotates the wood.

Something passes between them like a thick, black sound.

"What was it like to build a fire with him?" Walter says.

"We usually had more wood than this."

"I've got more than this."

"I was thinking of me."

"How much do you have?"

"Enough."

The word stays in the air and when it disbands, a feeling of desolation hangs around them. A car alarm erupts before being silenced. A distant dog starts its operatic scene before it disappears.

They talk about nothing for a while. Jack, a guy they used to hunt with, bought a large piece of land in Montana. One of his sons was in a bad car accident, lost his left eye. They talked about the rare occurrence of snow last December. They try to get something going between them. It dies out. They search again.

They rotate the wood.

They are caught in the night's cough, in its phlegmy haze.

"Usually the night before," Collins says. He sits on the back porch steps. "On the 23rd, I'd go over to Dad's and we'd have a glass of whiskey together." Collins picks at the dead skin of a callus on his hand. "Do you know what? That damn fire was only ever about Esman Bigler to him."

"Wilvin's Essie?"

"Dad went on one date with her first when they were fifteen, supposedly, before she fell in love with Wilvin. One date. Late at night, the conversation always went to Essie. How much he loved her. How Wilvin had stolen her."

"How have I never heard this?"

"One date. Took her to get a hamburger or something. And Wilvin says he only did that because he liked one of her friends. But even that didn't matter, because Big Essie only ever wanted Wilvin."

Walter stacks the sweetgum branches by the shed. They're done.

"What do you think? Did Dad love her?"

Collins rubs at a leaf of a potted fern with his forefingers.

"I think he wanted his life to have been different. That's what she was to him at two o'clock in the morning with whiskey."

Something mute bounces off the trees and fence, resonates so deep that Walter can't recognize it.

"What?" Collins says.

"Nothing."

They separate the wood into two piles. Walter stacks his by the shed then helps Collins carry his to the truck.

He dumps an old beer can filled with rain water on the smoking fire until it's nothing but mud.

By nine o'clock on Monday night, Phoebe still isn't home. Instead of calling her, Walter puts on a pair of pants and gets in the car.

He finds her car parked further down Calhoun Street.

He circles the block three times, tracing her trajectory.

Her car is in front of a three-story, stone-colored home surrounded by a low, trim hedge. Cast-iron cresting lines the top of the mansard roof. In the porch rocker sits a Santa holding a koozied beer while Mrs. Claus rides a sleigh in the lawn.

The humor collides with the haunted grayness of the windows. Walter parks two houses behind her on the opposite side of the street and cuts the engine.

Everything pulses beyond the car door. Walter turns off his lights, drops down low in his seat. He is taking root in an uninhabitable corner of the world.

He feels a faint vibration in his chest bone. Infrasound has been known to cause feelings of awe, fear, unease, disorientation. At 18 hertz, sound can be similar to the resonate frequency of the eye, cause optical illusions.

One might hallucinate his wife standing in the second floor window, carrying a child that isn't hers. Or he might mistake a four-limbed, dog-like animal racing behind the bumper of his wife's Volvo.

The front door of the house opens. Walter catches something in the muscles surrounding his words.

A woman in a pink warm-up holds the hand of a young girl, drinking a juice box. They climb down the porch steps. Neither of them is Phoebe. They wait at the bottom of the steps. A man in jeans and a navy sports coat follows. He is not Phoebe. The man locks the door, checks it, then joins them. The three of them walk around the corner of the block.

Walter turns on the car just enough to crack the window.

The stagnant night air gives no relief, except now Walter is certain he's being watched. She has found him, he thinks, and looks down into his palms as if it holds a wafer of truth.

There is a harmony now to the sound Walter feels in his chest. Two sticks rubbing together.

Walter slowly turns his head. He decides to lie about none of it. He is waiting for her.

Walter turns his whole body to look.

It is a woman in a suit and slippers. She is outside of the house where Walter is parked, holding a bag of trash to take to the curb. She frowns in front of her shotgun, camelback home with no holiday decorations.

Walter starts the car. The engine silences any sound he felt before. She drops the bag and walks back inside.

Walter keeps his lights off and pulls away from the house. The only other spot is a half a block up. His view of Phoebe's car is completely obscured.

He sits back in his seat and tries to listen for her coming. The sound of heels on concrete. The chatter of car keys.

There is a buzz. Against the door frame a fly does its Cadmean dance. Walter fists it against the window. Something destructive moans inside him.

The sound of night bugs ticking offbeat surrounds him.

Things peak before they fall. Leaves before the bare of winter. From five to seven every evening, the kidneys reach the height of their function then drop off.

It's almost midnight when Phoebe gets home. Walter is in bed, trying to seem asleep. Low breaths, relaxed eyes.

He listens to her have a glass of water from the kitchen faucet. She brushes her teeth. In their room she unzips her clothes. The sounds grow nearer despite her.

Walter lies still. The word glory comes from the Greek word doxa, meaning expectation.

There is a helpless, widening happiness on the other side of that fire. Walter tries to picture it as Phoebe climbs into bed, shifting the mattress and the sheets. The dip inevitably pulls them together. Their existence, determined by metal box springs.

When she becomes still, he tries harder not to move.

Fire removes one of nature's most essential properties.

Gravity stands no chance.

THE FLAME IS BOTH DANGEROUS and pure. Idolatry is easy.

On Tuesday afternoon, Walter is finally able to get a straight answer. Mr. Marny's body is still unclaimed at the morgue.

"What will happen to it?" Walter asks.

"You're not hearing this from me," a nasal-voiced man says, "But we've had some bodies here since the 80s."

No other details could be released.

By four o'clock, Walter drives fast down Canal Street with Boon in the passenger seat. "We need a good find," Walter says. "I saw this construction site last week." He's hoping to make it there before the workmen leave.

The building is an old dance hall, the insides gutted. Walter can see the arrangement of the tables, the podium for the band. There are lights strung up from the low rafters of a small, packed jazz joint. Phoebe leans into him. The smoky, throbbing heat makes her hair stick to the sides of her forehead, releases the starch in her white-collared dress. Sound bounces off the brick walls and finds way into their bodies. Walter should be at home, studying for his med school exams. They sip stiff drinks flavored with a little lime. Let the ice sit on their tongues. Dip their bodies into each other, even on the offbeats. The music shifts and they have no problem keeping up. They find their rhythmic stride.

"I can't dance to the music," she says, laughing with thick-liquored breath.

"Me neither," Walter says. But they do.

Walter walks to another window, cups his hands and looks in.

Opened walls and electrical wiring. Weathered floors, broken tiles. The place is stripped. "I was hoping for scaffolding outside. That's what we need," he says.

They try the doors to the building. Locked.

"Maybe there's a window we can get through?" Boon says.

"We're not breaking into abandoned buildings," Walter says. "Check the dumpster."

"It's all plaster and sheetrock."

"Dammit," Walter says as they walk back to his truck.

"Turn around," Boon says as they drive down Claiborne Avenue. "I saw something."

Walter pulls into the parking lot of the Home Depot. A sad row of Christmas trees limp against the side of the store. Their branches so thin, Walter can see the trunks.

"Pull up over there," Boon says, pointing to the shipping pallets stacked near the side entrance.

"They aren't throwing those out, Boon." In fact the dumpster is almost on the other side of the parking lot. They're the reusable kind, made of oak or cedar.

"Don't turn off the car," Boon says.

"What? No," Walter says. He begins to pull the car back around.

Boon undoes his seat belt and opens the door while the car is moving. "Even just two would be good."

"I'm not getting arrested for stealing Home Depot's crates," Walter says. "Boon."

It's too late. Boon is already hoisting two over his head and into the back of the truck. Walter scans the parking lot and watches the door. A woman hauls a potted plant to her minivan. A man walks out with a toilet seat and blinds. He doesn't see any orange-vested workers.

"Come on, Boon."

Boon lifts a stack of three pallets over his head, lets out a whoop and drops them in the back of the truck. "Go. Go. Go," he says jumping back in.

Walter rushes the gas, and they skid away.

They roll down the windows and whoop all the way out of the parking lot.

"Awww-dog," Walter hoots and slaps the side of his truck. "You happy?"

"What? What? Like you've never stolen anything before?" Boon says.

"First time," Walter says through a smile. Rhythmic energy converges into one surprising moment that faces the future. Walter is the unexpected blow of the derby mute. He forgets to drive pass Calhoun Street. He's the improvised solo. And when he pulls up to his house, Phoebe's car is nestled in their driveway. Life's syncopation.

"Put it here," Boons says and holds out his arm. Walter bumps his fist. "Don't make a habit of this," Boon says as he walks to his truck. In a fatherly tone, he adds, "You know, you can't steal fire."

A string breaks. A drum stick drops. "Yes, sir," Walter says. He doesn't have the heart to tell Boon, they can't use stolen wood in his bonfire.

O N THE CAR RIDE OUT to Wilvin's on Wednesday night, Walter is trying to remember the smell of Phoebe's night cream. He can liken it to nothing.

He drives along I-310 towards Vacherie to check on the wood that some of his crew has dropped off at Wilvin's, see if any of it needs to be seasoned.

He drives through a numb, gray twilight. The trees line up like tombstones. Their inscriptions are written in verse. It is yourself you see.

Walter can recall the metallic smell of a body's open cavity. The first mesquite log he lit. The marsh in summer. But not the face that leans into him every night.

When Walter pulls up to the one-story yellow cottage, he isn't surprised to see that though the grass is cut, the yard still seems overgrown. The house leans slightly to the left and is twenty years past needing a new paint job.

There are a few things Walter can be sure of when visiting Uncle Wilvin.

One is that upon entering his house there will be a clear, plastic spit cup somewhere in sight. It is very likely that he will regrettably catch sight of dark brown tobacco gunk floating. He will hold his breath when he passes it, because worse than the sight is the smell.

The second is that on some table in the first two rooms there will be an unfinished game of cards, probably bourré. Either a neighbor will have had to leave early or a granddaughter will have had work; whatever the reason, he will be invited to sit down and finish the game with the old man, might be the last he plays.

Walter is sure at this point that the games have never been started by anyone. They are set out as-is to lure someone naive with a little time on his hands. And once caught, Wilvin can keep a game of bourré going for a long time. Longer than anyone would want to shuffle back and forth cards, tossing penny bets on a table.

Walter walks through the back door to the smell of leather and fresh tobacco. He spots the first spit cup on the hallway bookshelf. Something has changed. The plastic is wrapped in duct tape.

Wilvin calls from the living room, "Grab a beer and pick up this hand that Joe Grisby left this morning."

Sure, Walter thinks, this morning.

In the kitchen, a dying bulb struggles to stay lit. It buzzes dark, comes alive, fades back down. The dishes are clean and neatly stacked in the rack. The table is old but wiped free of crumbs. And in the refrigerator are two six packs, a stick of butter, some casserole in a dish, white bread and cold cuts that Walter can tell Wilvin bought for tonight.

Walter pulls up a chair and picks up a crappy first hand. He watches Wilvin eat a handful of pretzels. He checks his face for clues of his cards. When Wilvin eats his whole face chews: his temples, the tips and lobes of his ears, his cheeks, they all roll. Walter notices his freshly pressed khakis and colored shirt, along with his signature Domino Sugar baseball hat that he wears too big so his ears fold slightly outward. He's a small man, but doesn't give the slightest impression of frailty.

"What do you got, Walt?" Wilvin taunts. "First hand, you're gonna want it to be good."

Anytime Walter plays, Wilvin talks to him as though it is his first game. Walter tosses down a five of diamonds.

"Well, that ain't great," Wilvin says.

"No, Sir. No it's not."

Wilvin takes it with a two of spades.

Walter looks around at the faux-wood-paneled walls with taxidermic plaques: a boar's head, couple bucks, mallards. His eyes land on the worn-out accordion retired over the couch. It hasn't been played since Essie passed. When Wilvin has had enough to drink, he sometimes says, it plays on its own.

Wilvin picks up the mug next to him, Mickey Mouse and a white-gloved smile. He spits in it.

"I got some bad news," he says and shuffles the deck.

"There's no wood. It was a decoy for cards."

"There's wood."

"If you take my money this round I quit."

Wilvin deals. "Alma broke up with Boon this afternoon."

Walter checks his cards. A queen of hearts and a seven of clubs is his best bet. "Another proposal?" Walter slides two pennies towards the center. "Should we put money on how long until they make up?"

"Think this time is for real." Wilvin checks his cards. He discards all five, gets a new hand. "She's still in love with that Jonny guy from down the street. Found out he was getting a divorce."

"Poor kid," Walter says. "Good news for us though. We'll have him do all the sawing this weekend." He combats Wilvin's ten of diamonds with his queen of hearts. He wins the trick.

"I don't think that's how it's going to go down. Heard it got pretty messy on her front lawn."

"Took it that bad. What'd he do?"

"Not Boon. Alma. She's got that Doucet anger."

"Lucky for us, I think we're on the side where the honey locusts go," Walter says. He shuffles the deck.

The discard pile grows.

"How's the car?" Wilvin asks.

"What?"

"Your car. Collins said you were having some trouble."

"Did he." Walter gets up to get another beer. "It's fine."

When they moved on to whiskey, and Walter has lost twenty-six cents, they go out back to see the wood.

Wilvin has lined up the logs and leaned them against the house. Branchless Christmas trees.

It's not much, but it's big. Long logs of cypress, pine, elm. They're large enough to use as support beams or the base. Dry enough to cut up and use throughout.

"Nice," Walter says. He pulls a measuring tape from this back pocket and writes down the lengths. He'll take what needs to be cut and leave the rest with Wilvin to bring on the twenty-fourth.

"What'd my mom used to say?" Wilvin said, patting one of the logs. "...So habitual you can't tell it from love..."

"Not sure, Pops." Walter checks the backs of the logs for insects since they're leaning so close to the house. They seem clean.

"Do you know who I cheated on her with?"

"You on Essie? No?"

"Yeah. You remember Donna?"

"No."

"Yeah you do. She was the woman from the bank who gave y'all those hats."

Walter only sees thick ankles perched in heels too small and greasy crowns that smelled of onions. "Really? Her?"

"That's what marriage does to you. Makes you want women like that."

Walter tries to pick up one of the larger logs and nearly drops it into the house. "Gonna need a hand."

"I don't regret doing it, but I regret Essie finding out. It didn't change the way I felt about Essie, maybe made me love her more. But how do you explain that to a woman? Hell, it was crap with Donna. But you can't get a woman to believe that once it's done."

"Donna?"

They finally manage to hoist one of the smaller logs up and half carry it, half drag it to Walter's truck. The rest they're forced to leave.

They sit in low lawn chairs with metal frames and yellowed plastic bands.

Wilvin leans back in his and watches the sky. "There was such sadness and hate in her...you don't want people angry at you when they go out."

"I'd never," Walter starts to say about Phoebe, but stops.

Wilvin's lawn is mowed up to the tree line. No fence. For almost a mile, just crowded trees and brush. Unowned land. A silent inanimate world. So mute, so merciless, it's situated beyond time.

"Do you want to know the last thing my brother said to me?" Wilvin says. It sounds as if he's going to choke on something. He thumbs out a blackened wad from inside his lower lip. He flicks it into the grass.

The chair clicks as he leans back. He drains his beer.

He doesn't have to say. Walter knows the type of things Dad said as he sunk from this world.

It's almost ten o'clock when Walter gets back to New Orleans. He takes the long way home down Carrollton to St. Charles. He takes a right onto Calhoun Street and drives all the way down to Magazine Street.

He doesn't find her car.

110

He makes a loop and goes slower down the street, passes the nested cars, the endless Santas taking flight.

The thought of telling Collins, Wilvin. It closes his breath.

Her car is not there. He pictures it hidden in a garage. The house with the Who Dat sign. It has those windows she likes, the ones that open out.

He takes a left on Coliseum towards home and that's when he sees his secret weapon.

He sits there for a while just staring at it. An unruly, fading force with roots ripping up the sidewalk, the lawn. Its branches, dark, dull grey and no longer sprouting leaves, thrash in the cool air. It has the final burst of an octopus from the depths of the sea, the falling tail of a caught alligator, a tidal wave crashing down.

The tree is dying. It's only a matter of time before it has to come down.

Walter parks his car and gets out. He smooths his wrinkled shirt back into his pants. He casually walks up to the door rehearsing a smile.

Nobody answers when he rings the bell. He rings again.

A couple, mid-forties, maybe older, answer.

"Good evening," Walter says.

They stare at him blankly.

"I'm Doctor Walter Doucet."

"Is everything alright?" The wife says. She looks over Walter's shoulder.

"Everything is just fine. I live down the street." Coliseum is a long street.

"Do you need help?" The wife asks.

"Possibly," Walter jokes.

They both look at him, confused.

"Your tree is dying," Walter says.

"What kind of doctor are you?" The husband asks.

"Oh no, a nephrologist. Not a tree doctor. But your tree is dying." Walter nervously rubs his hands together. It seems as though they've inched back farther into their home, closed the door a little more.

"If someone trips on your sidewalk because of those roots, they can sue you, probably for a lot of money."

"Are you thinking of suing us?" the man says.

"No, not at all. I'll take the tree down for you."

"No," the husband quickly says, "No, thank you."

"I don't mind," Walter says.

"We'll hire someone, dear," the wife quips.

"I'll do it for free." It sounds more desperate than Walter intended.

"Why?" The couple say in unison. "Why do you want our dead tree?"

It is a pecan tree.

There is nothing better. Walter wants to say, pecan wood is a hardwood. It has a high combustion heat value. It's easy to split, easy to burn. It doesn't smoke heavy. It doesn't pop or throw sparks. It smells of nuts and vanilla.

It burns for a long time. Long enough for Walter to become victor.

Walter caves and tells them about the bonfire, the rules. All the while he's checking along the base of the porch for an outlet where he can plug an electrical cord. He thinks of fitting his plastic goggles onto his face and revving the engine. The shake the chainsaw makes when the metal teeth hit the bark. Wood chips flying. He'd take the branches down first, then work from top to bottom. It'd be ceremonious.

Before he knows it, he's telling them about Collins, about Phoebe's parked car on Calhoun Street—

The wife has taken his hand into hers and is patting it. "We'll have our guy come on Friday afternoon, if you want to stop by then."

"Really? Thank you." Walter shakes their hands. "That's so kind of you." He shakes their hands again. "See you Friday," he says.

For a second, the most fragile branches of life contain him. They warp and weft to support him.

On his way home, he calls Boon. No answer.

There is an unfinished sound in Walter's house. Like someone recently rang a bell or hit a gong. The vibrations haven't left yet. The slightest, still audible. The intangible, brushed.

He finds Phoebe asleep in bed. Her face tucked quietly into itself. Her body rises with each small breath, then returns.

Walter leans down and kisses her cheek.

Hyacinths.

THERE'S SO MUCH UNCERTAINTY WHEN a bonfire is first lit, when it starts to crackle. The heat and the smoke build. The more divided substances ignite faster than the larger ones. And there's a mixture of panic and exultation as the fire climbs up the tinder to the kindling to the middleweight and tries to stay there.

There is such a small window for it to catch before dying out.

And if it starts to fail, grown men try to feed it with their own breath. Desperate resuscitation.

Walter stands under the showerhead until the hot water runs cold. He thinks of the year his fire had six men on their hands and knees fanning the fading flames. He'd used too much heavyweight wood and not enough lighter wood to heat it.

He shaves, combs hair. It's almost noon.

In the kitchen, he plates the cold scrambled eggs and bacon Phoebe left for him. He makes a fresh pot of coffee.

He and Pierre sit on the back porch. Walter eats and Pierre finds a squirrel to chase. He's forgotten to put down the Brazil nuts.

He calls Boon. It rings then cuts to voicemail.

"Hey, kid," he says, "Just wanted to check. See how you were. Understand if you don't want to talk about it. But give me a call. Want to tell you about a pecan tree. OK. Call me. Bye. Bye."

He's barely hung up when the phone rings.

"—Heard your boy's gone," Collins says.

"Gone where?"

"Wilvin said he's gone."

"What are you talking about?"

Pierre breaks into a run, circling the yard and barking after a squirrel.

Walter claps his hands trying to distract him.

"He broke up with Alma," Collins says.

"She broke up with him."

"And now he's gone, moved back home. Guess it's just you and me. The trick up your sleeve is pulled."

The squirrel has run under the porch. Pierre squats by the stairs and yelps. "Move on," Walter says to the dog, nudging him with his foot. "He wasn't a trick."

"He had access to wood. You start carting him everywhere."

"He kept showing up."

Pierre has found loose lattice and wiggled his way under the house.

"Well, he finally went home. Lost pup gave up—"

The dog starts to bark when he can't find his way out.

"You're such a fucking loser and you don't even know it," Walter says. He hangs up.

Walter drives out to Boon's boudin stand off of Veterans Boulevard in Metairie.

When he pulls into the parking lot, Bayou Backyard is boarded up. The stand is nothing more than a small shack. The sign with the gator holding a pig to its mouth is gone. The door and windows looks like they're prepared for a hurricane. There's a fresh graffiti tag, Miss D, or maybe it's a P, Hunts You. Walter remembers when it was a sno-ball stand, can even see some of the lettering now that the boudin sign is missing. There's still the metal plate in the ground from the bucking horse ride for kids.

Walter peeks in a window. The tables and benches have been removed. In the back, the refrigerator door is open, nothing inside. The shelves, bare.

It's as if Boon was never there.

Walter sits in his car and stares at the stand. He doesn't know where to go.

He thinks of The Bank on Felicity Street. They might have reclaimed lumber to spare.

Walter finds himself calling Claudine, leaving a message, "Claud, It's Dad. I'm going to the place we got your shutters. Just wanted to see if you needed anything? If you wanted to come?"

Walter drives slowly to Felicity, waiting for Claudine to call.

She doesn't. The Bank has nothing. Walter is nothing but emptied out crawl space.

How long does it take for a kidney stone to dissolve? It depends on composition and burden. It could be a few days or a few weeks. Longer.

Walter is back where he started. In front of the house on Calhoun with the plastic alligators pulling the pirogue. Alligators communicate using infrasound when trying to mate. Walter parks in front of a light post, plastered with signs for guitar lessons and lost pets.

Phoebe's car.

He sees it. He's having trouble acknowledging that fact.

It's across the street, curled in a driveway.

Walter's basic biographical information dissolves in a fluid of the past.

The first percutaneous nephrostomy description was published in 1865. The patient, a four year old boy, died. No further attention was given to the doctor's procedures until the mid-1950s. Walter can't remember what year Walter was born.

A car taps the horn behind him. He puts on his hazards. The horn again. He pulls to the side of the street, cuts the engine.

The house is a simple Georgian. It has no shutters on its windows.

The only holiday decoration is a pine wreath with a red ribbon on the front door. What man hangs a wreath?

Walter realizes there is one similar on his house.

In the Illiad, Homer communicates two Trojan leaders' utter loss of manly power by having fish fight to eat the adipose tissue surrounding the men's kidneys.

Walter is nothing but lost perirenal fat. Is there a sign for that? Lost. Maybe torn from flank. Possibly devoured.

The porch light goes on and Walter braces himself. I will fight him if I have to, he decides.

Nobody exits. It may just be an automatic timer. All of this will shut off on its own.

The topoanalyst in Walter is making a map, a mental lay of the land. Are the shelves cluttered or neat? How large is the bathroom? Are the lights burned out on the back steps?

The chimney filled with creosote?

115

Is there a drawer with a false bottom? An armoire, a secret, a grave?
How else will he invade?

He notices the lamp waiting in the front room window. No shadows cross in front of the sheer, closed drapes.

That light is watching him with an open eye. It is mocking his prolonged pursuit of the futile.

He calls to the light,

I am here, the Vestals, the Druidesses, Inghean au, the Breochwidh.

My fire is lit and guarded.

I am born of flame.

Walter sideswipes the garbage cans as he pulls into his own driveway. In the garage, he tugs the chain of the light so hard it falls. The bulb shatters on the concrete floor.

Walter crunches on the glass as he fumbles in the dark for the ax. He takes it from the nail hanging on the wall.

He rips off the sheet covering the kitchen table from Vacherie. He drags it with its rotted legs and loose screws out into the backyard.

In the glare of the floodlight. The one Phoebe installed to deter intruders. Walter waits for each thought to appear from the shadows. And when it does, he holds the ax over his head and brings it down as hard as he can.

The satisfaction is fleeting. He wants something more.

He hacks until the wood is nothing more than fibrous fillers. Until it's not even worth it.

There are pieces of wood in the grass, in his shoes, in the dog's water bowl.

With ax in hand, Walter stumbles onto the back porch.

He lies down in a deck chair. He feels the water of his body evaporate into the night.

When Walter wakes, the sky is a deep morning blue. A cold dew soaks through his clothes. He's shaking.

He fumbles with the lock on the back door, nearly kicks it open.

Phoebe is in the kitchen. "What are you doing?" she says over a cup of coffee and the paper.

Walter shrugs and pours himself a glass of tap water. He drinks it all and then another.

"Claudine told me to tell you," Phoebe says, "that she got your message and she's sorry she forgot to call you back."

"When did you talk to her?"

"I called her last night about some drapes she wanted. Did you sleep outside?"

"I was working on the fire." Walter makes his way upstairs. "Are the girls coming tomorrow night?"

"They left this morning," Phoebe calls after him.

"Merry Christmas," Walter mumbles.

"What?" Phoebe says. "Did you say something?"

Walter gets in bed, falls back asleep.

When he wakes, it's almost one o'clock in the afternoon. The house is empty. He calls Boon.

This time, he picks up. His voice sounds small.

"Where y'at?" Walter asks. He watches the rain puddle along his driveway. The drain is clogged.

"Morgan City."

"What are you doing there? Did the wood from your sister get here?"

"Nah, Boss. The rain's held it up somewhere. I'm at my mama's right now."

"Sorry to hear about Alma."

"Yeah," Boon clears his throat. "Pretty rough."

"You okay?"

"I'll get there."

"If you're still at your mom's and you need the wood dropped off here—"

"I'm really not sure about the wood." The texture of his voice has flattened.

"I passed a construction site on Dauphine yesterday. Looked like scaffolding. You interested?"

"Not really." Boon clears his throat. In the background, Walter hears the banging of pots and a woman's voice. "Take care, Boss." The way he says it sounds misplaced, like a Wagner's meat market attached to a gas station.

"I'll come get you—" The phone goes dead.

Walter waits in front of the pecan tree for two hours. He's rung the bell six times. No one answers. No one has come to take the diseased tree down.

He thinks about going home and bringing back his chainsaw.

He gets out and goes up to the tree. He pulls on a lower branch to see if it will come down willingly. It won't.

He opens his trunk and finds only a hammer. He hits it a couple of times against the tree. Nothing happens.

Collins calls. Walter doesn't pick up. Collins doesn't leave a message.

He waits until the sun sets. Until hunger and night force him to forfeit.

The mind's images are elastic.

Walter parks in front of the house on Calhoun. The drapes are drawn in the front room.

Impalpable shadows of Phoebe's upper body are projected from where she sits on the sofa.

Where else does time live if not compressed in space? What else is space for?

Walter gets out of the car. The back of her head faces him.

He moves halfway up the sidewalk and stops under a tree. He looks at the trunk and the leaves. He has no idea what kind of tree this is, what kind of wood it bears.

Walter wants to steal this man's tree.

He watches Phoebe's shadow drink from a glass, set it back on a table. He waits for someone else to join her.

When he sees him, what will he do?

Walter is overcome with a fearful sensation of dying. He turns back towards the car.

Finds himself in his bed.

To be gained, must it be lost? No. That is impossible.

The simple law of of of—

Entropy, energy inefficiency, direction of time—

Everything is immemorial. Nothing can be recollected.

WALTER STANDS ON THE LEVEE in Vacherie and watches a smog slip over the top of the river. He drinks his coffee from the Circle K. One small boat makes its way up the quiet water. Dawn pushes the night sky up and lowers the moon. It is almost six in the morning. Walter is the first to arrive. The road is dead.

He's pulled his truck onto the grass at the bottom of the levee. The wood is piled high in the back. It will take a while to unload it. He's hoping someone else shows up soon.

He watches the steam rise from his cup. He listens to the caw of a bird looking for its mate. He finds himself searching the windows of the house.

Walter knows which pieces to cut with a point on the ends and which ones to blunt. He'd watched Dad do it while he threw a ball against the side of the house. He knows how to cut the bark of a log to season it when there's not enough time. He watched Grandpa do it while he fed a small fire out back with sticks. But there were things that weren't passed down that Walter wishes had been. Grandpa could tell a log was too wet to even bother just by looking at it from ten feet away. Dad had a place he called his joie de vivre. It was someplace north of the Atchafalaya Basin, and he never came back empty-handed.

When the light in the sky begins to find color, Walter puts on his gloves, pats them to release sawdust, and then begins to unload his truck. The larger pieces of wood he'll have to wait and do. The rest he can try.

After a few minutes, he starts to sweat. His heavy breaths are visible in the air. It feels like hours of work and most of it is done when he sits down on top of the levee. But it's been less than an hour, and no more than three loads of smaller pieces of wood have been brought up.

He forfeits until more men arrive.

Soon Walter sees a truck making its way down the road. It's got the same grille and front tires as Boon's.

He jumps to his feet. "Hot damn," Walter says out loud. "He did it."

The back of the truck looks like it's piled high with what Walter guesses are the honey locusts from his sister.

"The kid's come through." He tries to think of something funny to say, tease him.

He finds himself waving his arms over his head. He slides down the levee doing a little dance.

The truck makes the final turn and comes into clear vision.

It's not Boon's truck. The flatbed is filled with metal tubing tied down with tarp, not trees.

The truck gives a honk. The driver waves then moves on.

Walter trudges back up the levee.

The early sun clouds over and a chill sets in. Walter gets in his truck and turns on the heat. He puts his gloved hands up to the vent. They never put out a bonfire. It was always watched until it went out on its own. Grandpa and Dad put lawn chairs up on the levee once everyone went home, including Wilvin, and waited. There were times Walter and Collins joined them with sleeping bags then lawn chairs of their own. Walter wishes he could remember what they talked about on those nights. At the time, it was just men enjoying their whiskey, and what was important about that?

He puts his head back and dozes off in the warmth.

He jerks awake to the sound of tapping on the glass.

It's Uncle Wilvin holding up a fresh cup of coffee for him and a big goofy grin.

Walter rolls down the window.

"Ya slept right through it. It's the 25th. It's over. You missed it."

Walter looks over at the bed of Wilvin's truck. Harnessed down is the wood, the support beams. "Who helped you?"

"I know people," Wilvin jokes and climbs in the passenger side. He lets out a grunt from the cold.

"Is Boon with you?"

"He's gone, boy," Wilvin says.

"He'll be here." Walter puts on some old Opry country station for Wilvin. "I wasn't expecting to see you until later."

Wilvin sits there silently for a few minutes, then says of his brother, "He's still here. I feel him. That son of a—is still here."

They both force a laugh.

Wilvin sips his coffee. "My dad used to line up almost every piece of wood he gathered across that front yard. Then from the top of the levee, he'd watch it, wait for it to take a pattern of its own."

"I remember that," Walter says as the vague image comes back to him.

"Just keeps getting passed down, doesn't it," Wilvin says. "An action repeated. A different outcome sought. Delirious revelry, I tell you what. We are all swamp mad."

Same damn thing every year.

This is the last year, Walter promises himself. The last damn year he comes to this place. He's been saying this for the past twenty. He saws a wedge in a willow log, fits a smaller piece into its cut groove. He pauses to zip his fleece, pull down his camouflage hat. In the distance, passing somewhere north of them, a rusty freight train fumbles towards the smoke-billowing chimneys of petrochemical plants.

He remembers asking Dad, when he was six or seven, "What's the point of spending so much time building something, just to burn it down?"

He hears the grinding saw reply.

Walter is handed another cut log to fit in the pyre. "You heard from him?" a cousin asks.

"Not yet," Walter says.

"What's he doing?" another cousin asks.

"Not sure," Walter says. He watches the road for his brother's sports car.

"Maybe this year it's just one," Tut says with a pat on his back.

"Get me a beer, will ya?" Walter says.

Walter checks his phone. No messages. He starts in on another willow log. Slowly his pyre is taking shape.

At the bottom of the levee, the women set up the tent and tables for food.

Large boys in hunting fleece and scruffy faces haul loads from the back of pickup trucks. Someone brings up the ladders. A small group of men gather on the levee, camping out on orange coolers. Collins's crew.

One of them mouths to Walter, "Where is he?" and points to his watch.

Walter shrugs. Collins is late. No surprise there.

When the men aren't looking, Walter checks his phone again, no messages. He goes to dial Collins's number but stops. He puts the phone back in his pocket.

As Grandpaw used to say, "You can't put out water with fire."

"Thought you chickened out, C.," Tut teases. "Scared we gonna whoop ya?"

Walter turns to find Collins climbing the levee in a pair of khaki pants, a light blue polo, and suede topsiders.

"It's almost three," Walter says. "Where's your bonfire?"

"You nervous for us?" Collins goes to tackle him, but gives a tight bear hug instead. Walter twists uncomfortably in his grip. "Just be nervous for you." Collins taps him on the shoulder with a light fist.

"Where is it?" Walter asks, looking at Collins's parked sports car, no bonfire wood in the back. "Why are you all dressed up?"

"It's coming."

"When?"

Collins ignores him, starts making his rounds. Walter returns to grinding a three-inch groove.

"You're not cutting deep enough," Collins comes up from behind him. "Logs are gonna slip out."

"I know what I'm doing." Walter pushes the saw back and forth against the wood.

"You never called me back."

"I did," Walter lies. "I tried."

"Your boy here yet?"

"Not yet."

"When?"

"Later."

"The girls coming?" Collins shakes his empty beer can, tries for a last swig.

"Nope." Walter sucks in the cold air through the side of his mouth. Pain shoots through a rotting molar. He does it again. They aren't girls anymore, they're grown women with lives. They have better things to do. But what if he does finally win? All those years they had to watch him be a good sport, shake his brother's hand, his Dad's, humiliated by a fire that burned too quickly, wasn't big enough. His daughters, lit in their Christmas colors, looking more disappointed than him. "Shit." He's sawed the damn piece of wood in two.

"Too deep," Collins jokes, tapping his fingers on his can.

"Where's your bonfire, Collins? Is this a joke?"

Collins doesn't respond. Walter fetches another piece of wood. His crew steadily hammers beside them.

"Is it?"

"God, she doesn't age," Collins says. "How is that?"

Walter realizes Collins is talking about Phoebe, who stands near the table of eggnog and jambalaya. Walter can sense Collins pitting their wives against each other. In her tight red turtleneck and gold bell that jingles between her breasts, Phoebe is Christmas all wrapped in a sweater.

Last year Beccalyn looked like a melting, southern snowman in a white, tight jumpsuit of sorts. Her dull brown hair piled in curls on the top of her head.

Walter scans the crowd for Beccalyn. "Where's your wife?"

"She's got the flu."

Walter finds Collins's daughter, Eleanor, a carbon copy of his wife, though slightly thicker, standing next to the food table. Remy races around her legs.

Then there's Phoebe with her short, blunt blond hair, releasing her staccato laugh, all the world turning slightly below her. Walter wins.

"You're a lucky-ass man," Collins says.

"Will you stop."

A sudden anger grips him. An anger so intense that he thinks of driving over to the man's house, maybe shaking the life from him, maybe knifing him. But Walter doesn't know who he is. He feels even more pathetic. He keeps his eyes on Phoebe, waits for her to look at him, at the best bonfire he's ever built. She doesn't. She doesn't know he knows. He tries to swallow the anger, tries to picture his stomach acid gnawing it to nothing.

A sweet and bitter smell arrests him.

"What jackass already lit it?" Collins crumples his can, teasingly tosses it at Walter. It taps his thigh, and he ignores the drops of beer on his jeans.

Walter searches the sky for smoke.

Somewhere upriver, a bonfire is burning.

Collins is telling his joke. His crew sit on small piles of wood they've brought. Two of them hunker on an orange, plastic ice chest. They laugh like they've never heard it. They are good men.

Walter cuts into the last side piece. His crew is almost done.

"What's that joke of Dad's?" Collins asks him.

"I don't know."

"Yeah you do."

"It was a rhyme, and I don't remember it." Something about age and piss and being golden.

Collins's son-in-law, Waylon, finally arrives. He pulls up in a truck blasting Zydeco, their pyre in pieces strapped to the bed. Me-oh-my-oh. His camouflage pants swing out the door in a foolish hop. Stains splotch his T-shirt. Collins takes one look and gives him a half-hearted fist thrust. Walter can't help but smile. Just when Collins thought he'd picked every last piece of low country lint from his monogrammed sweater, his daughter goes right on and marries some backwater Cajun, the swamp still dripping from his mouth.

"Alright." Collins's crew slap their gloved hands against their legs and rush the truck. Around the side of the car comes Collins's grandson, carrying a large, round metal tray of some sort. Two men help Collins carry up the base.

"You think right here is OK?" Collins asks him, though Walter knows he'll put it where he wants.

"Sure," Walter shrugs.

"Farther down," Wilvin says. "Unless you want these fires catchin' each other."

Collins ushers the men down with his head.

"What kind of wood is that?" Walter asks, because it's a pale khaki and smooth. Not willow or pine. They drop the base. "That's a lot of work if you sanded it." Collins ignores him.

Tut holds up two pieces of wood, points to their tower's crown. "Walt," he hesitates. "Some of it's damp."

Walter grabs the wood, pats it to be sure.

"Well shit, Walt," Collins says. "Wet wood is the only kind that doesn't burn." A few of his men laugh. Some of Walter's crew laugh too. Walter forces a puh.

"I got some more cane in my truck?" Tut says, but the cane that sparkles and pops is for decoration.

"No, I'll find something," Walter says. He heads down the side of the levee toward the river.

Along the batture, he searches for dry pieces of driftwood. There aren't many. The wind moans like an old man waiting for life to release him. Walter pulls back up his fallen hood. A noisy skein of geese erupts. Without thinking, he lifts an imaginary shotgun, aims, shoots. The sound explodes between his tongue and tonsils, fills his cheeks with air. Something small and dark drops from a deep pocket in his memory.

From the top of the levee, Dad sends down lit kerosene-soaked cotton balls, "Dyin' Birds." Walter sees him now, racing back and forth in his wheelchair, a small blaze between his fingers, ready to roll. Then Dad disappears over the other side with wheels clicking, foot pedals snapping, metal bending. The sound is so real, Walter races up the levee to help him. But the snapping is not a foot pedal folding or metal bending out of place; it is the sound of clamps and hinges securing wood.

As quickly as if they are toy logs, Collins's crew assembles their bonfire. Each log seems to slip into perfectly cut grooves. Every angle neatly tucks into another. In a matter of moments, Collins's crew has done just as much as Walter's has since dawn.

"What is this, Collins?" Walter stands downhill, looking up at him. "A bonfire-in-a-box?"

Color creeps onto Collins's cheeks. He kicks at a crawfish hole.

Walter steps closer and looks at the wood, sanded and sculpted two-by-fours. "You bought it ready-made?" He doesn't know why he cares, but he does. "You bought your bonfire."

Collins stares, dumbfounded. "So what?"

"Congrats, you just killed a hundred-year tradition." Walter thinks of getting in his face when Collins's crew starts to cheer. Nobody pays attention to him. They clap as the last of their tower clicks into place. Walter realizes it's no taller than his, about twelve feet. Unable to contain his excitement, Walter starts to clap. He gives a whistle of his own, slaps one of the men on the back. Four sides. Collins's tower is only four sides. Walter has him beat.

With pride he barely recognizes, Walter climbs to the top of the levee, stands next to his feat. He slides the pieces of driftwood into the crown with his crew whistling. The first face he searches for is glowing back at him.

Phoebe's entire self seems to take in the site of his pyre. Walter squirms into a boyish, self-conscious grin. Phoebe gives him a thumbs up, detached from any sentiment, then politely turns to talk to a thick-legged relative in a cartoon-covered sweatshirt. Tonight, not even that can shift the ground from beneath him, because soon she will see. When Collins's is but a wee pile of cooling ash, his will still be burning.

The sun sets like smelting copper. Walter watches the billowing breaths of industrial stacks surround them. The WCKW Radio Tower, just shy of two thousand feet, looms over all Vacherie. In the distance, a fire truck makes its safety rounds along the levee as ignition time nears. Tut brings him a Coors in an old Mardi Gras koozie. They knock cans, take a few sips in silence.

"The Doucet boys set Vacherie ablaze," Collins says it like he's reading a headline.

"There's your rhyme," Walter says, but in good spirit.

Tut and the crew remove a few pieces of wood from the side and begin to fill it with gut. Scrap lumber, broken pallets, shavings, sticks.

"Where's your gut?" one of them says.

"I have it," Walter says, heading toward his truck. He also has a bag of cinnamon-scented pine cones to surprise Boon.

"Hell of a bonfire," a neighbor says with a firm handshake.

"The best is yet to come," Walter assures him.

Walter opens the door, picks up a piece of oak from behind his front seats. He holds it against his face, tries to smell the space between the bark and timber. Someone is watching him. He slowly lifts his eyes, through the passenger window he looks directly onto his grandparents' porch. Dad, an origami bird folded in a rocking chair, ruminates on cut tobacco. His jaw rotates in one endless motion. The skin on his face seems to sag from the bone, regenerate, sag some more. This is Dad crying. This is why he's crumpled. Walter remembers Dad flicking a bottle cap at him, saying, "Get out of here, you pansy-ass," but with a wavering voice. The open car door makes a sound, and he is gone.

Walter searches for his breath. He glances up once more to find the vine-laden porch, collapsed and empty. He realizes his lips are quivering. He rubs them together, tries to pinch them calm. Who is he? Who is the son of a bitch? He wants to yell to Phoebe, but nothing escapes his mouth. He clutches his bags of gut and watches her flit around the crowd.

Then out of the corner of his eye, he notices Collins's crew pulling sacks, filled with something small and lumpy, from the trunk of his sports car. His stomach drops so hard, he's sure the ground has shifted. Collins's crew carries the bags to their tower. They slide the metal tray in the base and begin to unload.

Bagasse clinkers.

The mill boilers' gold.

Fire that will burn for days.

"You're a cheater, a cheat," Walter has thrown down his bags and is racing up the levee to Collins. He picks him up by the neck of the shirt. "Who the hell sold you that?" he demands. When Collins says something cocky, he pummels him to the ground. Walter takes a swing and it smacks Collins's left eye. The next, square on the jaw. The next... none of this happens.

Walter waits with his bags at the bottom of the levee for someone to help him. His shoulders hunch from the weight, a cold sweat sits on his skin.

In the distance, dim lights swell like votives on the river's altar. The night sky, a grotto, and the water, mouths murmuring haste, desperate pleas in the form of common prayer. Our Lady, Our Lady. Walter stands atop the levee, his lips move in unison. It's almost time.

"You feelin' alright?" Wilvin's hand comes down on his shoulder.

"What? Yeah. Just taking a break."

Wilvin hands him a beer, then joins the rest of the crew in dousing the tower in fuel oil. The smell surprises Walter with comfort.

Below, in the dusk, the people's faces appear bleak. He senses Phoebe's gaze upon him but is too scared to see for certain. Walter shamefully wishes that whoever he is, Collins doesn't know him.

"How do you want to do this?" Collins says, because Dad always gave the signal. "Light on the count of three?"

This time Walter really does get close to Collins's face. "Why couldn't you just build the same fire that you've—" he stops, worried the choke in his voice might be heard.

Collins pulls back, laughs uncomfortably. "I can't build that type of bonfire." He seems honestly surprised that Walter doesn't know this. "None of these guys could." Walter wants to feel relief from this, but it doesn't come.

The smell of sweet cane on Collins's gloves tightens around Walter's throat.

Someone is singing Silent Night.

The others join in. He hears Collins next to him. Walter looks wide-eyed at Phoebe who calmly watches him. Her lips move, but he knows that she is just mouthing the words, that she can't sing in public. He knows this and it means nothing.

He takes the lighter fluid from Tut and splashes the sides of his tower.

He digs his grandfather's lighter from his pocket.

He sings a verse.

Red chasing white interrupts their song. Walter stops.

A fire truck with blaring lights pulls onto the levee. A man in a blue shirt, red suspenders gets out.

Collins rushes down, ushers the chief to the side.

The two men talk.

"Bullshit," he can hear Collins say. His gestures grow angry.

Walter releases a sigh into the flashing fires of joy. And he knows. The old man wind blows towards town.

And he is saved.

Walter gets a beer from a cooler. He walks down into the crowd, stops by the table for a styrofoam bowl of jambalaya. He makes his way around, confidently saying things like, "Maybe this wind will die down," and "must be my old man up there," or "he can't stand to see us do it without him." He points to the sky when he says the last one. People laugh, smile, pat him on the back. Good sport, Walter.

He glances up at his pyre, tall on the levee. Its entirety is the pure point of the flame, when color gives away to invisible vibration.

People seem in good cheer. Just kids complaining about being scared to use the bathroom in the house, as they should be. There's talk about one neighbor hiring a lawyer if the condition of the house doesn't improve.

Some people talk about lighting the fires anyway. "They're gonna arrest us all?"

No, Walter thinks, just my brother. Light away.

Nobody does.

Walter has made his way through the sixty or so people and he still hasn't found Phoebe. He walks down the road a ways looking for her car. The road is so still the parked cars seem ready to lunge. Phoebe's car isn't there.

He walks back up to the top of the levee for a better view.

In earshot of both the crews, Collins says, "Where's your boy, Walt?"

A few of the men make taunting noises.

Walter goes up to Collins, puts his arm around him, and pulls him close. In his ear he says, "You're just like him. That's why he left the house to you. So you'd have some place to live when you're old and alone and everybody's left you."

Collins pulls away and tries to laugh. He plays it off like Walter has told him some dirty joke, "Nice one," he says so the guys can hear.

Walter watches something quickly pass across his brother's face, then it's gone. Collins pats him on the shoulder. "Nice," he says.

The call of the fire can become so desperate, the need for destruction so blinding, a man will burn down everything just to get at one.

Walter takes one last look at his pyre and leaves.

Walter's car crawls down Calhoun Street. Every house on the block seems to sing with light.

He goes to the house. Lit in the front room is Phoebe, sitting on the same sofa as before. Walter watches her back. She sits there stiff; occasionally, she looks down at something.

There is a howl to the night.

Walter gets out of the car and walks up to the front door.

He rings the bell. It closes his breath.

No one answers.

He rings it again. There is a synaptic change, a hole opens.

It is filled with the sound of shoes clapping towards him.

"Walter, what are you doing here?" Phoebe says through a crack in the door.

"I want to know who lives here."

"Nobody lives here."

"Who?"

She opens the door wide. "Come in."

Walter walks into the front room, filled with mahogany furniture covered in deep red fabric. He goes to the next, a dining room table with eight chairs. A banquet table holds a silver tea set. The china cabinets are empty. The next, a stainless steel kitchen with cast-iron pots on the stove. The last, a small powder room, hidden under the steps. The walls painted a royal blue.

"Who lives here?" he tries to sound calm, collected.

"No one. I'm putting it on the market."

He sits on the sofa where he's watched her sit. His shadow stretches up the wall, covers a tapestry with a fox hunting scene. Phoebe sits in a Queen Anne chair across from him.

"So you've been showing it?"

"Well, no. Not yet. I come here to sit. Think."

"No man lives here?"

"What? No. She's dead and he's in a nursing home. The children live out of state. The McCullers. My dad sold them this house when I was a teenager. I used to go with him to show houses. Pretend I lived in them. Upstairs there are tiny doors in the window frames that store things. I wanted to live in this house. I begged him to let us live in this house."

She begins to blur into bayou water, run down over the wooden floors.

"How long have you been coming here?"

Phoebe pauses. "I got the listing about a month ago."

"I thought," Walter starts to laugh. "I thought—" His eyes tear, squelch whatever was rising. "We'll buy it. Do you want to live here? How much is it listed for? Who cares. Do you want to buy it?" Walter gets up and crosses the room. He picks up the mantel clock and taps on the face. It's an hour fast. He sets it back in its place. He combs his hair down in the mirror, straightens a crooked painting on the wall. He acts like these things are his.

Phoebe leans on the arm of the chair, folds her face into her hand. Her coif is flattened on one side. The skin under her eyes has begun to gray. She wipes at them. Smooths her skirt.

She looks past Walter. In a shaky voice she says, "I don't want the house now. I want it then."

He can tell that she is trying to keep her jaw poised. Her eyes are so burned out by something, Walter is scared to took at them. He might fall in, never be able to climb out.

"But I can't give you that," he says. His voice betrays him. He wants to tell her something about what remains. Something about cooling embers and building back up what can return. How sorrow is not the opposite of joy. He sits on the sofa and takes her hand. All that comes out is, "It's not my fault."

Her hand slides from his. "I know that, Walter." The way she says his name is unfamiliar. She hands him the word as if returning it.

Walter looks down at a stain on the worn rug, about six inches in diameter, a burnt brown. Next to it is a rip, possibly from a family pet. They know these types of markings, of unknown origin. He doesn't know how to tell her that.

His eyes, ears, and mouth try to close him off to avoid escape. His breath presses against his chest.

"Go home, Walter."

"I don't want to leave you here."

Walter's eyes move along the oriental patterns that spread out below their feet.

So loud is the clicking of the clock's hand as it counts to infinity.

"Go home, Walter."

He goes.

All sounds have been sucked into the sky, except the guttural trill of the phone.

It's five-thirty in the morning. Walter reaches over Phoebe in their bed to pick up the call. It's the nursing home.

Phoebe's mother had a fall in the bathroom. She's been taken to Ochsner Hospital.

"This is the beginning," Phoebe says as she buttons the blouse she had on the day before.

Walter gets up and makes coffee.

"Do you want me to come?" he says.

"She's scared of you."

Walter watches QVC reruns. An automatic sprinkler system. Pedals to work out while you sit on the sofa. The only knife you'll ever need. He waits for Phoebe to call with updates.

The presents stay under the tree all day, wrapped. It doesn't matter. They both know what's in them.

By late afternoon a storm rolls in from the Gulf.

Wilvin calls. The fire department needs them to take down the pyres. Safety hazards.

Nobody from the crews wants to do it on Christmas day. Walter drives out alone.

When he gets there, Collins is standing on the levee, facing the water. His pyre isn't there.

Dark clouds tumble overhead. It is the color of dusk at two o'clock. The wind whips up their hair and shirttails.

Walter walks up the levee and stands next to his brother. Collins doesn't say anything.

Walter sees that Collins's pyre blew down over the other side. What's left is lapped by the water's edge.

 Collins watches it.

Walter faces the house. "You want it? You gonna fix it up, put your pretty little wife—"

"It's over," Collins says. He doesn't look at Walter. "Beccalyn wants me gone. Had me move my stuff out last week."

"Where have you—"

"With a buddy of mine."

"Who?"

"Golf friend, you don't know him."

"You can stay with—"

"Nah, I think I found an apartment in Kenner." Collins turns to look at the house, "I could fix it up."

"—I didn't mean it, what I said—"

"—I'll probably demolish it, sell the land," Collins says.

Walter puts his arm around him and pats his back. "We could light mine."

"The fire department would be out here in a second."

"I know," he says, but still holds out the lighter.

"I'd stay and help you take it down," Collins says. "But I promised Beccalyn I'd—"

"Sure, yeah, go on. I got this."

Walter waits for Collins to say "I'll call you" or "we should go hit a round next week" or "grab lunch this Friday?"

Collins walks slowly down the levee with his shoulders hunched and doesn't look back.

Walter clears out a corner of the shed. He finds some tarp balled up in a corner, shakes out the mouse droppings. He finds some more plastic in his truck.

The wind dies down. The calm.

He hauls the ladder out. Standing on it, he whacks the crown with a two-by-four until it hits the ground with a thud and rolls.

Piece by piece he undoes his pyre.

He carries each log down the levee, through the overgrown grass and to the back of the house. The larger logs he pushes and kicks towards the shed.

He puts the wood on the tarp, ties down the other sheet on top of it. He cuts slits in the plastic to help release moisture.

Wet wood is of no use to him.

Walter drips with sweat and his muscles shake with exhaustion when he brings trash bags up the levee to get the last of it. His hands are blistered. A pain shoots through his legs and lower back. The body's entire blood supply passes through the kidneys every five minutes.

Slowly, he begins to bag the guts.

He remembers what Dad said when Walter asked him that day, why they spent so much time building something just to burn it down.

"Think we can rebuild it, I guess," he said.

"Can we?" Walter said.

The saw.

Walter stops to catch his breath. He watches the river. It is clear of any boats. The sky is dark enough that the water seems to go in various directions all at once.

He thinks of how in 1811 or 1812, because of an earthquake and thrust fault, the river reversed its course. It did the seemingly impossible. It flowed backwards for a brief period of time.

He listens to it rush by. A lone bird calls out to an empty sky.

Can we? Walter says to himself.

He thinks he can hear the wind find way through the open rafters of the house. But it is just the hollowed-out rustle of a breeze through branches.

Can we?

We try.

ACKNOWLEDGMENTS

I WOULD LIKE TO EXTEND my gratitude to the following:

Bruce Rutledge and everyone at Chin Music Press. The remarkable writer and editor David Rutledge. And Carla Girard for her beautiful designs.

The incomparable Brian Gresko, Ryan Matthews and Patrick Callihan, and the many others who were willing to read various drafts.

My most admired artists for their support: Patti Clarkson, Howard Altmann, and Richard Greenberg.

Those I worked with at Posman Books, especially Becky, Faye, Garrett, Lance, Grace, Dan and Andy.

The Kimmel Harding Nelson Center for the Arts and The Vermont Studio Center, for their generosity and the writers that I met there.

Janelle Collins and *The Arkansas Review* for publishing an early version of this story.

Endless thanks to my family and friends, especially my Mom, Dad, Michael, Arthur and Nanny.

A most humble and sincere thank you to: Ann Hood, Helen Schulman, Jackson Taylor, Paola Corso, Brad Richard, John Travis, and Anne Giselson.

And of course, inadequate words for my daughter, my husband and our writing group.